The Holly & The Ivy

Other Books by B.C. Deeks

Witch in the Wind
Stories of Chance Romance

The Holly
&
The Ivy

A Frost Family Christmas Story

By

B.C. Deeks

Copyright 2013 Brenda M. Collins

Publisher: WriteAdvice Press

Cover Designer: Kim Killion at http://www.hotdamndesigns.com

Editors: Linda Style at http://www.EditingwithStyle.net, and Mr. Ted Williams, Freelance Editor

Formatting: Anessa Books

ISBN: 978-0-9878918-7-7

Paperback Version

Baby Found in Nativity Manger

A newborn girl was abandoned this past Saturday evening at the Frost Family Maple Farm as temperatures dropped below freezing and the annual Frosty Frolics activities got underway.

The baby was bundled in several layers of blankets when found by an event organizer in the nativity manger. The infant is healthy and safe today, under the care of a local family in Carol Falls.

CFPD Chief Rufus Slayton says his officers are working closely with Social Services to reunite the child with her mother. They are appealing to anyone in the vicinity on Saturday evening to contact them.

Chapter One

The wind shrieked its fury as the sleet pounded down on the streets of Carol Falls, Vermont and crystallized into a clear, crusty coating on anything that stood in one place for more than a minute.

Officer Joey Frost sat in her patrol car, in the parking lot of the White Pine High School, sipping coffee and watching her hometown turn into a wintry mess. She'd decided to start her evening shift early, as soon as the light snowfall had turned to sleet. After five winters on the job, she knew the Carol Falls Police Department would be inundated with calls from holiday shoppers with vehicles stuck in snowdrifts.

Now that night had fallen, everyone with any sense was waiting out the storm tucked under a warm blanket at home listening to Christmas carols. Her eyes were gritty with strain as she swallowed the last dregs of her lukewarm coffee. She rolled her shoulders and blinked hard a couple of times.

Joey grew up in a two-story clapboard

farmhouse on the hill directly above the school and loved everything about her town, even the weather. However, any tourists planning to spend their holiday up the highway at the Stowe ski resorts were going to be royally ticked when they saw the condition of the slopes after this ice storm. She shoved her patrol car back into *Drive* knowing that, like most years, at least one of those tourists would have let enthusiasm override common sense. In this weather, there was no telling who might have skidded off the road this time.

With only five days left before Christmas Day, the town sparkled with festive spirit, despite the weather, as the snow caught on the pretty wreaths and clusters of boughs decorating Spruce Street. She could name the family living in almost every house as she drove by. Some she'd gone to school with, others worked on her parents' maple syrup farm, many more operated local shops and businesses. Her grandmother used to say, *Small towns are filled with neighbors, not strangers.* Gran would know, since the Frost family had been part of this small town for five generations.

At the end of the square, Joey slowed for the traffic circle in front of Lincoln Village Green, a four block green space named for one of the town's founding families. The towering Christmas tree at the north end was a splash of red and green against a background of sleet. Beyond, Red Bridge Road took her through a covered bridge that had separated Carol Falls from the rest of the world since 1803.

She tapped her radio mike on.

"Taylor?"

"Here, Joey," the police dispatcher responded.

Joey raised her voice to be heard over the noise of the wind tunneling through the bridge structure. "Town's secure and deserted. I'm heading out to check conditions on the highway."

"Ten-four."

Only an idiot would be out on a night like this, but she'd learned that skiers didn't always assess risk at the same level as ordinary people. Which was why *she* would take this risk at least as far as the ramp to I-89.

As the minutes ticked by, the strong gusts howled down the open highway nearly blowing her vehicle off the road as they whipped past her. She rolled her fingers on the wheel to ease their stiffness and squinted at the black ribbon extending into the darkness ahead of her. It made her feel like she was launching into outer space. Her back and neck were beyond pain from the long, tough shift and her head screamed at her to call it a night. She was ready to listen when a shadow streaked into the road ahead and froze in the beam of her headlights. Two red eyes glared at her.

Joey jumped on her brakes, fishtailing despite her slow speed. Her heart pounded for a few seconds and then settled. When the animal didn't move, she rolled the patrol car to the shoulder, and carefully stepped out. Sleet shocked the warm skin of her cheeks, like the simultaneous stabbing of hundreds of sharp pins. In one smooth movement, she pushed her parka out of the way and unsnapped the holster on her duty belt. She approached the animal with her hand poised over the butt of her weapon. In weather like this, it could be a coyote looking for prey. The pack might not be far behind.

She squinted as she closed in on it, and finally

determined it was definitely a dog. A Labrador retriever, maybe with some border collie mixed in. And the poor thing was wet, and very cold from the way it was shivering. A chilled cloud formed when she puffed out the breath she'd been holding.

"What are you doing out here tonight, buddy?"

The poor beast sat on its hind haunches and hung its head in misery. She could sympathize as the tip of her nose tingled, warning her it was about to freeze. The dog was almost all black, although some patches of his wet fur had frozen into gray clumps. Ignoring the discomfort, Joey dropped to a crouch.

"Not feeling too happy are you, buckaroo," she said softly. If her brothers saw her now, they'd kill her for taking such a chance, but she had a feeling about this furry guy. "If you're cold, I have a nice warm car over there with a blanket to curl up on." Normally, she'd report the sighting to Animal Control in Waterbury, but they wouldn't come to Carol Falls in this weather. She couldn't leave it to die from the elements. Or worse, risk an accident the next time it ran onto the road.

The dog inched forward and offered his paw. She shook it and then rubbed his ears, and finally, slid one hand down his neck to look for a collar. No luck, he'd slipped it in a moment of foolhardiness or was another dumped dog. People thought they could abandon a domestic animal in the country and they'd somehow return to the wild. Most times, they didn't survive.

"Okay, buddy boy. Let's get out of this weather." She eased to her feet. "Come!" she commanded.

The dog didn't need a second invitation to

settle into her heated vehicle. By the time, she was behind the wheel again, he had rearranged the woolen emergency blanket, which she'd spread out to protect the back seat upholstery from his wet coat, into a cozy nest and fallen into an exhausted sleep.

Poor baby. She wondered if her mother would be willing to take in another one for the holidays. Although Sylvia Frost wasn't allergic to human babies, the canine variety was another matter. Thinking of babies, of course, reminded her she'd recently missed out on the biggest case to hit Carol Falls—well, ever. "Figures, stray dogs are all that show up when I'm on duty."

She glanced back at the sleeping mutt. "No slight intended, big guy."

With her focus back on the road, she continued to vent to her new partner. "I leave town for a training course and suddenly an infant shows up in the manger of a nativity scene. On my family's farm, no less." She'd laugh if the disappointment wasn't still so fresh.

Frosty Frolics was the town's kick-off event for the Christmas holidays, and was hosted by her family at the Frost Family Maple Syrup Farm. The event two weeks ago had been the first one to ever feature a live—and totally unexpected—infant in the manger. Another police officer, Erik Wedge, caught the case that night. He'd arranged with state family services for the baby to stay at the farm with her parents, under foster care, over the holidays. All before she got home from her training course. She was going to be really ticked if that case gave him an edge over her for the promotion to the new deputy chief position when, and if, the funding ever came through.

Joey allowed herself one heartfelt sigh, and pushed it from her mind so she could concentrate on her driving. She didn't get far before the headlights again caught something in their beam— this time on the side of the road ahead.

Flipping on the flashers, she coasted along the shoulder until she was close enough to confirm a dark-colored sedan angled in the ditch with its front wheel up to the axle in snow and mud. Was this where the dog had come from? Was the owner hurt? After a quick radio call to report her location, she was out of the patrol car, using her flashlight to scan the area for signs of life, human or wild. No movement inside the car, as far as she could see. Hopefully the driver hadn't disregarded the cardinal rule of survival—never leave your vehicle— and wandered off looking for help. If so, in a storm like this, whoever it was would be an ice cube by now. She picked up her pace but that didn't mean much when she had to fight the suction of the ankle deep snow pulling on her boots.

Suddenly, a series of colorful profanities exploded from the car's rear. The driver, looking more like a black bear due to his heavy winter parka, popped into view and threw an evergreen bough off to the side. He must've been trying to use it for traction. At least, he'd had the sense to dress for the severe weather. Joey stopped in her tracks, clutching the flashlight more tightly. She pulled her scarf away from her mouth and yelled for his attention, "Carol Falls Police. Do you need assistance?" The wind snatched her words before they reached the stranger. She trudged forward as he leaned into the wind and worked his way around the uphill side of his car. When they were a couple of feet apart, and he still hadn't looked up, she waved her arms to get his attention, afraid he'd bump right into her.

He immediately caught her movement and closed the rest of the distance. Even face to face, she couldn't see his features with his head buried deep inside his hood. He tried to say something but she still couldn't hear over the howling storm. She pointed to the patrol car.

His hood moved up and down, and he jogged back to pull a large canvas duffle bag from the trunk of his car. Despite the slippery footing, he moved with surprising agility for such a big guy— over six feet tall by several inches and with broad shoulders—even allowing for the bulk of his outerwear.

She took the lead back to the patrol car, following the path left by her earlier footprints. After her first few steps, it occurred to her that her back seat, where she'd normally put a passenger, was already occupied by the dog, who might be dangerous if disturbed. If it was his dog, it would be okay but she couldn't be sure of that at this point.

She considered her options as she listened to the stranger's footsteps crunching through the snow behind her, closing the distance. If he'd wanted to highjack her car, he would have tackled her by now, she decided, although she'd keep her guard up. When she popped the trunk for him to stow his gear, she noticed his parka and the canvas bag were military issue. He might have survived the storm without her help.

Once she was back in the driver's seat, she stretched across the bench seat to push open the passenger door. The dog sat up and barked, probably saying, Forget him. Turn on the darn heat.

Good idea. She unwound her scarf, pushed back the hood of her parka, jammed the keys into the ignition and got the engine going. Even in the short period she'd been out of the vehicle, the outside temperature had dropped the interior temperature below freezing again. A thin layer of frost coated the inside of the windshield.

She felt the seat sink as the stranger got in with a heavy sigh, so she turned to get a good look at him. He raised his hand, pushed off his hood.

Joey choked. "Fletch?"

She hadn't seen him for ten years, but he didn't appear much different. His hair was much shorter, but the same ink black of her memory. And that aquiline nose and strong jaw were unmistakable. But the lines etched on his forehead and around that beautiful mouth, hadn't been there before. Evidence of a harsher life, telling of things he'd seen and done since leaving Carol Falls that had seasoned him. It made her want to ask him about that life, where he'd been, had he thought about her at all.

His startling, glacier-blue eyes scanned her face, widened, and she caught a flash of something more than recognition in them. "Hi, Joey. It's been a long time."

Yes, it had been a long time. What was he doing in Carol Falls now? Joey wasn't sure she was ready for the answer. Maybe she should have left him and his car stuck in that snowdrift.

~~~

Damn storm. Fletch had known better than to head out when the warning was issued but he was so close, he just couldn't wait any longer. He would have made it, too, if he hadn't had to swerve for some damn animal in the road.

When he left the military police after his last tour in Afghanistan, he'd lined up a job with Boston PD but his starting date wasn't until spring when some guy retired. It was dumb luck that he'd heard about the deputy chief position in Carol Falls. Of all the places he'd lived all over the world as a military brat, that small rural town was the only place that had ever felt like home. Although, to be honest, his warm feelings probably had more to do with Joey Frost than the town itself. Fate was giving him a second chance to see if the one he let slip away might be interested in being found again. He'd taken the job as a three-month contract to find out. And here she was. He hadn't even made it into town yet.

Having Joey rescue him from a ditch in a raging blizzard was downright embarrassing, but, as he watched her scrape at the windshield like a cat trying to get outside to pee, Fletch felt his lips stretch into a smile. He still made her nervous, just like when they were younger and she'd blush every time she looked at him.

At sixteen, Joey had been adorable, with the long, white blonde hair and the gilded hazel eyes of an angel. Her hair was a couple of shades darker now, but still blonde, and still pulled into a pony tail showing off her beautiful face. His parents had let him stay with his aunt in Carol Falls to finish high school stateside while his father was stationed overseas. He'd worked at the Frost Family Maple Syrup Farm that first summer, where he and Jimmy Frost would hang out most evenings, playing guitar, sneaking a few beers or smokes, or just lazing around as eighteen year olds do.

Mrs. Frost would set out an extra plate for him

at meal times, as if he belonged at their table—like he was one of the family. Mr. Frost sat at the head of the table, with his eldest son, Garret, at his right, and his second son, Jimmy, at his left. Joey was the youngest of the siblings, and the only girl, so she sat next to her mother. Fletch was given the chair next to Jimmy, which put him directly across from Joey. The Frosts ate their evening meal together as a family—no excuses. And everyone had an equal voice, often at the same time, as they argued, laughed, talked and listened. As an only child, it was something he'd never experienced before or since.

Watching Joey now, Fletch wished they could go back to that wonderful time in their lives. *One of the best.* Fletch sighed. Except, this time, there would be a few things he'd do differently. When Joey first recognized him, he'd seen shock and surprise on her face, but underneath, there'd been something else. She wasn't all that happy to see him, and he felt a little stab of guilt. But, it was high school, damn it. He hadn't returned to Carol Falls since then.

Joey had looked at him like she'd seen a ghost—then quickly schooled her features into a stern mask. He couldn't just drop everything on her like a bomb. *Hi, Jo. I'm here to see if you want to come to Boston with me.* The whole reason he'd taken the temporary deputy chief job was to allow some time for courtship. To make sure it would be right for both of them. And to leave him an escape route in case he *had* burned his bridges with her because of the way he left town.

"Noel Fletcher. What are you doing back in town?" she asked, breaking the spell. She turned away from him to snap on her seatbelt. "You ignored me for the whole last month of high school. How could you do that? You were like part of the family, and you didn't even say good bye."

He heard the tightness in her voice and recognized it as lingering hurt. Apparently, her mind was still on the issue of his departure as well. She'd always been very single focused. It was one of the things he liked most about her.

"I, um, I can explain—"

He couldn't actually. Not off the top of his head, anyway. So it was a good thing he was saved by a movement in the rear of the vehicle. A big black dog was sitting on a blanket looking at him as if he might be dinner.

"What's with the dog?" he asked, grabbing the opportunity to change the subject.

"My new partner," she replied, her tone flat. "He's very protective."

He took in the wet fur coat but didn't contradict her, figuring the stray had just made up for running him off the road by saving him from answering her question—at least for now. He'd have to explain eventually though. Unless she'd changed, and he really hoped she hadn't, Joey could be a dog with a bone once she got something into her head.

"Great," he said, as Joey shoulder-checked, pulled a careful U-turn onto the highway and headed back to town.

Road conditions were treacherous, so Joey was keeping a careful, steady speed and didn't encourage conversation. He'd liked that about her, too, when they were teens. She wasn't one of those bubbly, fussy girls who'd chase any guy whose voice had broken. Maybe it was because she was so used to being around her brothers. Her very protective brothers.

Of course, he'd noticed the hot blonde running around the Frost farm in short shorts and a tank top, but, even then, he'd been man enough to know how to keep his hands off his friend's sixteen year old sister. He'd tried hard to think of her as a little sister. He'd succeeded for that whole summer, and almost all of his senior year. Until Jimmy asked him for one favor.

The police radio crackled to life. "Joey? Everything okay?"

Joey took her hand off the wheel only long enough to open her mike. "Ten four, Taylor. Just back in the vehicle with a passenger in tow."

"Need any medical assistance?"

"No, all clear here. I'm heading back to town with the driver."

She glanced at him then, and cocked an eyebrow. "Where were you headed?"

"Aunt Elle's. She's expecting me." His aunt was the only one who was, other than his new boss. The whole thing had come up at the last minute and had felt so right he'd just grabbed it without thinking it through. He'd asked his aunt to keep quiet about his return, thinking it would give him a better chance of wooing Joey. Now he was questioning that strategy.

She spoke into the mike again. "He's got relatives in town. I'm ready to clock out so I'll drop him off on my way home. But could you arrange for a tow truck in the morning?" She gave coordinates for the disabled car.

"I'll give Buckley's Auto a call. And, Joey, don't forget Chief Slayton wants everyone in tomorrow for the nine a.m. meeting."

Joey groaned. "Ten-four." And then gave her full attention to driving.

"When did you become a cop, Jo?" That was making him think he should have asked his aunt a few more details about Joey as well. He'd worried about a lot of things with this homecoming but her job hadn't been one of them. A police officer. Fletch rubbed his palms over his thighs. He didn't have much time to talk to her before they reached town. Should he invite her out for coffee now, before she found out what he was doing back in town?

"Going on five years now." Joey told him.

"I can't see your father going for it."

She looked at him and smiled. "Dad insisted I go to college first...in case law enforcement didn't work out. I think he was hoping I'd change my mind."

"Like *that* was going to happen." Fletch had no trouble remembering her old man striding around his property—energetic, dynamic, powerful. What he couldn't imagine was Harold Frost being happy about his only daughter becoming a police officer.

Joey chuckled. "It didn't. I went right into the academy after graduation."

"I assumed you wanted to stay on the farm."

"The farm was always going to go to Garret. I love it too, but it wasn't what I wanted to do with my life."

"Is the job what you expected?" Or had she done it to prove something to her family? He remembered how competitive she'd been with her brothers.

"I love it." She looked at him again, and the glow on her face left no doubt she meant it. "It was

Mrs. Hoadley who suggested it to me. Do you remember her from school? She was my ninth grade homeroom teacher, but I don't know if you would've had her for anything in your senior year."

The mention of high school brought a shadow across her face. His initial read on her was right. She wasn't going to let go of how badly he'd botched things up when he left town after senior year.

He'd seen her around the farm over the summer but that fall, he was sitting on the bleachers behind the school one day when he noticed a lone figure burning up the running track. He hadn't recognized her at first. Not until she came around the final turn, the late afternoon sun casting her in a golden glow. He'd admired the shape of her legs, the flat muscled abdomen visible below the sports bra covering her small rounded breasts, her neck straining forward from her strong shoulders. Then his gaze settled on her face and his gut knotted. Her jaw was clenched, her brows pulled together as she focused so intently on that line in the dirt, she was totally unaware of anything around her. Fletch was captivated as she stretched one long, slender leg out, leaned her torso over until nose and knee were almost touching, and flew over the finish like a thoroughbred trained to win. Even now, Fletch's heart pounded in his chest with the memory. He could never forget that moment— when he'd fallen in love with his best friend's little sister, Joey.

Fletch wiped the condensation off his side window with his sleeve and scowled as Joey slowed to enter the covered bridge leading into town. He'd run out of time to explain the situation to her. His homecoming plans were suddenly a whole lot more complicated than he'd anticipated. As they drove through town, the sleet began to let up and a few giant snowflakes started falling in its place. The surrounding mountains tended to cause sudden weather swings, he recalled. Carol Falls looked the same as when he'd last been here, but he wondered how much had changed under the surface.

Joey pulled up in front of his aunt's house before he was ready to leave her. She bent down to hit the trunk release so he could get his gear.

"Thanks for the ride, Jo. It was great to see you again."

"No problem. Try to stay out of trouble while you're in town."

She looked tired as he pushed open the door and started to get out. He couldn't resist one poke at her, for old times' sake. "If I don't, do you promise to arrest me?"

He saw the twitch at the side of her mouth. "I'll send Wedge to get you."

Remembering the little runt who'd followed Joey around like a puppy in school, Fletch had to laugh. "Don't tell me he's a cop now, too?"

A full smile lit her face. "Yup, and he's grown a lot since you saw him last."

Chapter Two

A plaintive whine emerging from the floor beside her bed startled Joey awake the next morning. After living in a working farmhouse her whole life, it had taken a while for her to adjust to the silence of her small bungalow on Fir Street, although, now, she couldn't imagine moving in with her parents again. She was groggy and achy from her long shift the night before, as she pushed up onto one elbow, leaned over the side, and came nose to nose with the dog. She flopped back on her pillows.

"Right. Dog. Storm." Her mind struggled to link the key pieces together. She really needed a coffee. "Dog. Storm. Fletch."

Her eyes popped open.

Crap. Did she pull Noel Fletcher out of a snowdrift last night? She shivered, but staying in bed wasn't going to help with this kind of chill. Had he said what he was doing in town? He'd never come back for the holidays before. What other reason could he have?

She threw off the covers and stumbled to the

bedroom window. The town was a picture postcard for the season, which was a shock after suffering through nature's wrath the night before. Every tree, car, fence—everything in sight—was encased in a thick layer of ice, and sparkling in the first rays of the morning sun. The snow was pristine white, still pure after its drop from heaven.

Joey yanked on her boots and winter jacket over her flannel pajamas and headed outside so the dog could take care of business. Intent on thumbing through the messages on her mobile phone, she pulled the front door shut with her free hand. A shower of ice daggers rained down on her from the eaves. She stumbled over the dog as she jumped away. He looked at her as if she'd failed in her duty to protect him.

"Get over it, bud. It's winter in Vermont." The temperature hovered around ten degrees below zero, but felt much colder because of the dampness in the air.

It took another half hour for her to take a quick shower, get dressed and find something suitable in her refrigerator to feed the dog. Technically it was her day off, so she pulled on her comfortable jeans and sweatshirt instead of her uniform as she pondered why the chief of police was calling in all the officers for a meeting. Had her promotion finally come through? Chief Rufus Slayton hadn't promised the new deputy chief spot to her outright if he got the budget approval, but there had been broad hints that she was the frontrunner. She'd put in the shifts, she'd closed files, she'd made him look good to the town. What else could be important enough to call an all-staff meeting at nine o'clock in the morning? It was an uncivilized hour for those coming off the evening shift, she thought with a yawn.

The car door moaned about the cold when she pried it open. Once she was inside with the heat on, the scent of oiled leather with a touch of cedar drifted around her. Like a conditioned response, long forgotten, her mouth watered and her muscles tensed. What guy smells exactly the same after a decade? Apparently Fletch did. He had his own unique scent. Not a soap or cologne. And she still responded to him like a cop to coffee. The memory of seeing him in her rear view mirror as she pulled away the night before made her squirm. She hadn't said, *glad you're back.* Or *see you around.* Or *can I nibble your neck later?* She'd dumped him on the curb and forced herself not to check if he was watching her drive away.

The dog rumbled his opinion.

"Well, I could have left him in the snowdrift on the highway like he dcscrvcd." She jammed the vehicle into gear. "It wasn't like he deserved a big welcome home hug."

A grunt from her passenger.

"Okay, I didn't welcome him back like he was practically one of the family, because he didn't act like one when he left without a word to anyone," she said, but couldn't convince herself. Now that Fletch wasn't sitting in her space using up all her oxygen, she could think straight. "I should have pretended I didn't recognize him. He'll probably tell himself I'm still hurt over a high school crush gone wrong and his ego will be all inflated." The heat crept to her cheeks as if it were yesterday. Stupid to be embarrassed after all this time. "He probably doesn't remember that part at all. When an old friend from high school comes to town, a normal person suggests getting together for a coffee to reminisce." The ache in her chest made her want to forget about their past. Another of her grandmother's favorite sayings floated up from her memory. *The past never stays where you think you left it.*

"Well, it looks like a ghost from my past has come back to haunt me."

Her canine companion didn't have an opinion on that one.

After parking in front of the police station with the hope that her meeting wouldn't take very long, she headed inside taking the mutt with her rather than leaving him in the cold car. She tossed her parka onto a hook by the door. Several figures were visible through the large glass window of her boss's office. She was about to be late if she didn't hurry. She walked over to the dispatch console, which was tucked into its own alcove off the main patrol room.

When Taylor Pope was hired late the previous winter, Joey had looked forward to having another woman as an ally around the station, especially one about the same age. Instead, Taylor was friendly to everyone, but close to no one. The woman was perplexing. She was everything a police dispatcher needed to be—calm, efficient and articulate, which was at odds with the unflattering, bohemian outfits she favored. The one she had on this morning was so completely shapeless she could be hiding half the town council under it and no one would know.

Joey pasted on her most innocent, pleading smile when Taylor looked up, then down at the dog, and back at Joey with her eyebrows raised. "I picked up the poor thing last night, half frozen to death. No collar. I've been calling him Buddy," she volunteered. "Would you mind—?"

"You can leave the dog with me," Taylor said, rubbing his ears. "And you need me to call Animal Control, right? And post the notice with the town clerk?"

"Yes, please. I need to get into the meeting."

"Okay, but you need to think of another name."

"Why? What's wrong with *Buddy*?"

"It's kind of masculine for a female dog," the other woman replied.

Feeling stupid for overlooking such a detail, Joey froze for a moment before inspiration hit. "It's short for *Rosebud*."

Taylor's usually placid face creased into a full-scale smile. "Works for me."

Joey shrugged and smiled too. Maybe they would become friends after all.

With Buddy in good hands, Joey pushed open the door to the chief's office, stifling a yawn with one hand. When five sets of eyes locked on her, she sucked in a breath and snapped her mouth shut. The office was on the small side, but was normally adequate for the team's rare staff meetings. Today it looked cramped. The two officers from day shift were leaning against the far wall with their arms crossed. They nodded a greeting. Erik Wedge had scammed the chair in the corner. He had it balanced on its two back legs, and she wondered how long the two spindles could support all that solid muscle. Like her, he was officially on his day off so he was dressed casually in dark blue jeans with a T-shirt and hoody.

"Hey, Joey. Late night?" he asked, his face the picture of innocence.

Joey didn't answer. Her attention was locked

on the man sitting directly in front of the boss—Noel Fletcher. A shot of adrenalin knocked the fatigue right out of her. Her boss eased forward, his bulk causing his chair to squeal for mercy, and rested his forearms on his desk blotter. "Take a seat, Frost. Let's get this show on the road."

Chief Rufus Slayton was her father's age but that's where the resemblance ended. Where Harold Frost maintained his tall, lean build by working outdoors, riding horses, skiing in the winter and hiking in the summer, the chief sat at his desk most days, drinking coffee, and then going home to his wife's hearty country cooking. Harold ran his hands through his hair when he was worried, but the chief didn't have any hair left to pull when his job got stressful. And, where Harold could charm the feathers off a chicken, the chief was a slow-moving, plain-talking, old school, country police officer, who was waiting out the last few years until his retirement.

She closed the office door and mirrored the posture of her colleagues across the room, forcing herself to look confident and relaxed. The briefing started with confirmation that the highway was closed for the next few days due to the blizzard. Joey stared ahead trying to figure out what Fletch was doing here. She'd been sixteen and in full hormonal bloom when he first showed up at the farm. She'd drooled from her bedroom window as he worked, often shirtless, in the hot summer sun. It had suddenly become important for her to apply a little powder to her nose and to brush out her waist-length hair every morning before she went down to breakfast. As a senior that fall, he'd been a heartthrob to the entire female population at school...and the grand passion of her young life.

Then he'd left without a word and broken her heart.

Her ear picked up a change in topics.

"I am happy to tell you that, for once, the budget talks ended on a positive note for Carol Falls. I was able to get funding for a new position, deputy police chief."

Her heart pounded against her ribs and a knot formed in the pit of her stomach. There was movement around the room, mumbling, a few glances cast her way. But instinct gnawed at her, something was off. She shifted her weight, crossed her arms over her chest and listened to the rest of the announcement.

"And I found the perfect candidate to fill it," her boss's voice droned on. "Noel Fletcher is a former soldier with experience as a military cop, and with Carol Falls itself."

What? Fletch was getting her promotion? That sneak hadn't said a word about it last night when she'd rescued him. Why hadn't he told her this was what he was doing back in town? And her own boss hadn't given her a moment's thought for the position. Fletch wasn't the only one who *knows the town* and is *seasoned in law enforcement*. She had proven herself over and over again for the last five years. And, unlike the chief's prize candidate, she'd done so as a member of this very department.

Bitterness burned through Joey as she locked her teeth together and focused all her energy on keeping her mouth shut. Still, disappointment and frustration smoldered and seethed until it threatened to boil over.

"Frost, I'm partnering Fletcher with you for now. I want you to show him the town."

Joey choked on this added insult. Offering her

up like a paid escort was not what her boss intended, but Wedge had a smirk on his face, and the corner of Fletch's mouth twitched before he could control it. Neither said a word. They both knew she was armed. She did *not* see the humor in the situation. If she wasn't good enough for the job, why should she spend her time showing Fletch how to do it?

"Sir, I'm sure Officer Wedge would be better suited to train our new recruit." The gloves were off. She might as well have called Fletch a rookie and everyone in the room knew it.

"Moving on—" the chief said...his way of saying it wasn't a negotiation.

Joey's training and experience made it possible for her to keep her face blank while she struggled to push her emotions deep within the cage she used to store them while on the job. Her boss didn't give her much time.

"Frost, where are we on the vandalism investigation?"

Carol Falls was typically a quiet mountain town that attracted mostly family type tourists wanting to tour the maple farms, visit the cozy shops around the main square, hike the local trails in summer and ski the nearby mountains in the winter. Crime in all the towns in the area generally consisted of nuisance calls. However, over the last few months, vandalism—mostly graffiti in nature—had been escalating and was now considered *a problem* by the town council, which meant the police were under pressure to haul someone in.

"The storm kept V*andal Gogh* out of trouble," Joey replied, using the town's nickname for their graffiti artist. "I gather spray paint doesn't dry well in wet, sub-zero temperatures." She wondered if the chief had used the sudden crime spree to justify the new position, as she finished with, "I'm still pursuing leads, sir."

He made no comment and nodded to Wedge to report on his primary case, the Baby Doe file, involving the baby abandoned in the manger.

"I was able to confirm the infant was not born where she was found, sir. Not anywhere near the Old Sugar Shack on the Frost property." The building was so named because it had originally been used by Joey's grandfather to boil the sap to make the Frost family's famous maple syrup. Now the old structure was only used to host events for visitors and guests. "The baby was several hours old when she was discovered and was born at another undetermined location."

The only humor Joey had gotten after missing out on the case was thinking about how uncomfortable Wedge would be investigating it. He grew up with little female influence, since his mother had died and older sister, Kate, had left home, both before he'd turned ten. He was mortally awkward talking to women about *pregnancy*, *birth*, and, God-forbid, *breast feeding*. When they were both at their desks at the station, Joey couldn't resist pretending to talk to a girlfriend on the phone about female issues just to make him squirm.

"So you haven't found out where the actual birth took place?" the chief asked.

"No, sir." Wedge hung his head. "I've checked around town, in Stowe, and even in Montpelier, to see if anyone remembers seeing an unfamiliar pregnant woman. Checked the bus terminals too, in case one of the drivers noticed someone. We don't have enough to support a warrant to approach medical facilities or professionals for a more official search of their medical records."

The police chief tapped his finger on his desk. "And the evidence from the scene?"

"I've checked to see if we could get anything on where the baby sleeper, diaper, and the rest were purchased but it's all generic—the kind of stuff you can get at any big box store in any city or state. So we're back to the quilt."

Before Wedge could continue, the chief turned to Fletch to clarify. "When the babe was found, she was wrapped in a quilt that looked handmade. If it is, it might be unique enough to give us a lead."

Why was he so freaking concerned that Fletch be brought up to date? Was he handing over the primo case, too...along with her promotion?

Her boss signaled Wedge to continue.

"No one in town seemed to sell anything like it and the merchants I asked believe it was stitched by hand, rather than manufactured, but couldn't say by whom. We photographed the quilt and then sent it, the baby's clothing, the diaper and everything else, off to state forensics for testing. There's no telling when we'll get anything back from them. For sure, not before the new year." He shrugged and looked around at his fellow officers. "Honestly, sir. I'm out of ideas. And nobody's talking."

"Would they be more open with a female cop?"

Joey spun to stare at the idiot who'd raised *that* question—Fletch.

The men could ask their own damn questions as well as she could. She swallowed her irritation so they wouldn't hear it in her voice. "I already have my own case, sir. You know we need to get the vandal case closed or the mayor will have a melt down—"

Chief ignored that and said, "Wedge, since you're taking your vacation days between Christmas and New Year's, would you mind giving Frost a shot at that file to see if she can break through the wall of silence?"

Wedge had a stupid grin on his face, happy to have an excuse not to work the case on his time off. "No problem, sir." His grin faded a bit when their boss added, "You take over Frost's regular patrols. Fletcher and Frost can buckle down on the Baby Doe and Vandal investigations immediately. I want both cases closed by the end of the year. Frost's right about Mayor Lincoln bein' on my butt."

Joey threw a confident smirk at Wedge. All she'd needed was a chance at that case. It didn't matter if her boss didn't believe she was good enough to be deputy chief. It didn't matter if the job was already taken. She didn't need the title to be the best officer for the job, and she could prove it. The only way the Baby Doe file was landing on Officer Erik Wedge's desk after the holidays, was *CLOSED*. And she didn't need help from Fletch or anyone else to do it. That gave her a little more than a week to figure out who the birth mother was, and why she'd abandoned her newborn in Carol Falls

Chapter Three

An hour later, Joey tapped her foot repeatedly on the worn hardwood floor of the patrol room, stopping—when she remembered—to take a bite from her roast beef sandwich. Since the first hour of her day had seen her lose her promotion, and get Fletch as her new partner...and new supervisor, Joey decided to focus on the only positive thing that had come out of the morning meeting. She'd even borrowed Wedge's notebook to get his more immediate impressions from the scene where the newborn had been found in the manger.

Erik Wedge's desk was beside hers and, with his strawberry blonde hair and baby blue eyes, Erik still looked like Prince Charming. He and Joey had started kindergarten together at the Carol Falls White Pine Elementary school, which was when he'd decided Joey was his princess. The romance ended abruptly in second grade when she broke his heart by deciding all boys were yucky. After that, they'd shared an uneven alliance. At various points in her dating life, Erik seemed to develop proprietary feelings toward her that she handled badly in middle school, and as best she could in high school. Now they were co-workers and friends.

As expected, Wedge had been thorough in his reports. He had logged every interview, whether he learned something useful or not. He'd logged every call to family services, including the one to report that Sylvia Frost, Joey's mother and custodian of the child, had taken the baby to the medical center as a follow-up to the initial assessment. There was a note that Joey's mother had started using the name, *baby Holly*, because the infant had been discovered as the choir at Frosty Frolics was singing Sylvia's favorite Christmas carol, *The Holly & The Ivy*.

She ran her finger slowly down each page of Wedge's neat handwritten notes to make sure she wasn't missing any of the details of the investigation. Because something kept throwing off her concentration. Was it the scent of leather and cedar irritating her nostrils, or just the prickling at the back of her neck? Why did the chief have to put Fletch in the desk right behind her? It wasn't like she couldn't walk across the room if they had to consult on some aspect of the case. She didn't need to talk to him anyway because she could solve it without him. Why hadn't she gone home, instead of staying to work on her cases? She re-read the sentence about the baby quilt for the third time.

With renewed vigor, Joey flipped to the front of the file again. She liked to approach an investigation like a puzzle, laying out the bits and pieces of information she'd gleaned from the file on sticky notes. She wrote evidence or facts on yellow sticky notes and her own unanswered questions on blue ones, and stuck them all over the top of her desk. Once she had everything in front of her, she took a deep breath, rolled her shoulders like she was going into a competition, and stared down at them. Another twenty minutes and she still had a desk full of blue and she was ready to crawl out of her skin.

Glancing over her shoulder she saw Fletch had moved into the chief's office and they were talking with the door closed. Might be a good time for her to slip out without him. She could run by the vet with Buddy to see if the clinic had a record of her with an owner listed. If not, since the highway was closed, the mutt was going to be around for a while and needed to be checked for vaccinations anyway. She collected her from Taylor and was reaching for her parka when Fletch called to her. She didn't bother to turn but waited for him...still facing the door to make it clear she was on her way out.

He stepped in front of her and rested his hand on the doorjamb, effectively blocking her escape route.

"Trying to run, Jo?"

His breath tickled her neck as he spoke, making her skin tingle.

She took an involuntary step away.

His lips curved into a smile.

She blinked and felt her cheeks burn. At five feet, eleven, Joey could stand nose to nose with most guys, but to glare at Fletch, she had to tip her head well back.

He kept his voice low. "Joey, I wanted to tell you last night—"

She took another step away and zipped up her parka with more force than was necessary. Even when they were teens, she'd been clumsy whenever she was around him. After the stress of this morning, his presence was making her crazy. "But you didn't, couldn't, whatever. I have to take the dog to the vet. What do you want?"

"I don't get why you're *so* upset."

She hissed out a breath. Could this situation get any more humiliating? "You're probably the only one in the station who didn't know I was up for the job you just got."

He stared at her. "I'm sorry, Jo. I had no idea. No wonder you're mad, but could we at least go out for a drink or something so we can talk?"

Talking wasn't going to change anything and he was now her supervisor. "I keep my work and personal life separate." She couldn't hide the edge in her voice, when she added, "May I leave now, sir?"

His lips narrowed into a thin line as he nodded.

In the background, Taylor picked up a call, listened, and then told the caller an officer would be there in a few minutes.

He still hadn't moved to get out of her way, so she called out, "I'll take it, Taylor. Where to?" Might as well, since she was at work anyway, and it would get her away from Fletch without looking like she was running away. "Billy Boy's. A drunk and disorderly."

Not a call she'd be anxious to grab under normal circumstances but this wasn't a normal day. "On it," she said, ducking under Fletch's arm.

"Not without me, partner," Fletch said, brushing her shoulder as he reached past her to grab his jacket.

"I'm driving," she said, her voice sounding weaker than she'd intended.

Fletch smiled. "Okay. I'll take shotgun."

Their destination was around the corner and two blocks down from the police station. Even though it was close by, carrying a drunk wasn't an option. It was a long three-minute drive, made in silence.

Billy Boy's Bar was not meant for tourists. It was a serious drinking establishment where the local men could have a brew, eyeball nearly naked waitresses, play some pool, and not worry about how many F* words they used in a single sentence. Twinkling fairy lights in the street side windows were barely visible through the grime on the glass and the plain wreaths hanging in each pane were more for hiding the patrons from prying eyes than providing any holiday atmosphere.

As they pulled to the curb, she recognized Sammy Lincoln, the mayor's son, standing on the sidewalk. Nearby, a slender young girl in an oversized parka was arguing with the bouncer at the door of the establishment. Stuffing her hands in her pocket, Joey stepped in front of her new partner as she approached the trio. She could hear the girl's voice rising.

"But I just want to take him home before he gets into any trouble."

The bouncer, who Joey knew as Zack, looked over at their approach. "Too late for that, doll."

The girl turned and her already pale face lost the last stain of color. Joey recognized her from the high school. Ivy Belmont lived down near the gas station a block or two east of the bar. A good girl. Her mother cleaned houses for a living, the Frost farm included.

Sammy, who'd been turned away from them,

swung around and, seeing Joey, stepped in front of the girl like a bodyguard. He lived on Maple Farm Road not far from Joey's parents' farm. She'd known him most of his life, babysat him for years.

"Hi, Sammy. Hi, Ivy," Joey said. She could feel Fletch's presence behind her. It was distracting, not being able to read his face, to guess what he was thinking. It could take months to years for two officers to develop a smooth, well-coordinated partnership. The first day was bound to be uncomfortable, Joey told herself, but she didn't believe it. Fletch was her supervisor, so it would definitely take longer, or never happen. She had to hope the chief meant for theirs to be a short term relationship.

Ivy stepped out from behind the boy and stood tall with her hands on her hips.

Joey wasn't fooled by the brave front. "Why don't you head home now, Ivy. Let us take care of your father for you."

She pushed her chin out. "He doesn't mean to cause trouble. He hasn't been himself since he lost his job."

"Ivy, your father's problem is a bit bigger than that," Joey replied.

"No. He was fine until the town council made all those funding cuts and he lost his job and his benefits, and his pension . . ." Her voice hitched so she pressed her lips together. So strong for a sixteen year old.

Sammy's face flushed. "My dad's an idiot. He doesn't get that his decisions hurt other people."

Joey wished there was some way she could fix what was happening to these two kids, already caught up in adult problems. "The mayor doesn't always get to make the decisions he'd like to personally. He has to consider what's best for the whole town, now and in the future. It gets really complicated."

Sammy wasn't interested in any excuses and crossed his arms over his chest.

Joey heaved a sigh. Nothing to do but focus on the issue at hand. She flicked a glance at Fletch, standing a few feet behind her, to see how he was reacting to the situation. She wasn't clear about their reporting relationship in the field. Was he still her supervisor? Partner? Only an observer? He wasn't giving her any signals so she decided to ignore him.

"Christmas is a tough time of year, Ivy. You go on and we'll bring him home to you safe and sound."

"Give me your word of honor." Ivy's voice was tough, demanding, but she pinched her lips together tightly to steady the tremor.

"I promise, Ivy." Joey replied. "Sammy, could you please see her home safely?"

Once they were out of earshot, Fletch finally spoke up. "You shouldn't make promises you can't keep."

"I don't. I'm going to keep this one." Then she took a breath. A new partner wouldn't be questioning her judgement on their first call together. He was acting like her superior.

"Christmas is hard for lots of folks, but that doesn't give him the right to cause trouble for other citizens," he replied.

Irritation sizzled at the back of her tongue but she controlled it. "In our town—for a father of five kids—we cut him some slack and help him through the rough times."

Zack, who'd been standing by, nodded his agreement and held the door open for them. "Sorry to bother you officers, but we were afraid Mayor Lincoln might show up for his weekly pool game."

"Thanks, Zack."

"Huh?" Fletch gave her a puzzled look. As an outsider, he wouldn't get the connections between the mayor and their Drunk & Disorderly.

"Our mayor hobnobs with his constituents at this end of town over a beer and a game of pool every week around this time."

Their boots crunched on the empty peanut shells as they walked over to the long, well worn wooden bar on the far side of the dimly lit interior. Oliver Belmont was holding himself up with one hand and waving his half-empty beer around in the other, giving a rambling and colorful discourse on why the town council, and its leader in particular, was to blame for his lack of employment and the decline of Carol Falls in general.

This time, Fletch stepped ahead of her, forming a human barrier between her and Belmont. In a flash of annoyance, it occurred to her that her partner might be trying to protect her in case the individual in question decided to throw the beer bottle. They'd be having a chat about that later. Supervisor or not. However, Belmont was well past the point of resistance when they escorted him out, each of them holding an elbow to keep him upright.

They made the journey to the Belmont home without further trouble since their back seat passenger had either dozed off to sleep, or passed out. As they neared their destination, all the houses seemed to need maintenance of some kind—they had shutters hanging askew, shingles lifting on the roof and paint peeling off siding—but his was in even worse shape than the others on the block. Keeping her voice low to be sure Belmont wouldn't overhear, Joey explained to Fletch that the Belmonts had lost their house and been forced into a rental in this, the poorest section of town. One or two of the homeowners had made a pathetic attempt at decorating for the holidays with strings of lights, some of which were burnt out, or cut out snowflakes hung in a window. The sight made Joey feel sad.

When they arrived, they escorted Belmont up to his front door, and then a scowling Fletch held him up, while she rang the bell.

"Your mother's working today?" Joey asked Ivy, when the girl answered the door.

"Yeah, she's taking on extra jobs while she can 'cause everyone wants their house cleaned for Christmas. I'm in charge." The young girl was acting the part of the mature woman of the house, but the relief was discernible under the surface when she saw that Joey had kept her word. Ivy briskly led the way to the sofa in the living room where Fletch could deposit her father. She had been a little overweight in the fall, Joey recalled, but now, she looked more like a starving waif, with her brown hair cropped short, and her tiny frame hidden in her baggy jeans and man sized hoody.

Joey stayed behind in the hall so she could take a look around. Just because she was sympathetic, didn't mean she would turn a blind eye if the trouble at home was getting out of hand. The kitchen was on the right, where she could see kids' drawings pinned to the fridge, reminding Joey that this had once been a happy family. The stove beside it was old but spotless and the linoleum floor was freshly mopped. A large oak harvest table took up most of the room, with Ivy's nine year old sister and the younger twins sitting around it making paper snowflakes. All three were frozen in mid-motion, staring at her with wary eyes. Beside them on the floor, a quilt was carefully wrapped around a sleeping toddler.

Joey's stomach clenched. She tried to reassure them with a smile but knew it was futile. There was little she could do other than ensure their safety and access to family services if it became necessary.

Harsh words coming from the other room grabbed her attention.

"There's my girl, Ivy. Too lazy to stay in school. Just up and quit. She'll be a loser like her old man."

Fuming, Joey spun on her heels and followed Belmont's voice, ready to cut off his cruel, spiteful words with her bare hands before the children had to listen to any more. Couldn't the man see what he was doing to Ivy and the rest of his family?

Belmont was upright but swaying, his eyes glassy and spittle collecting in the corner of his mouth. Fletch was towering over him, making the most of his greater height and strength without inciting a fight. If the older man had been sober enough to recognize the menace on Fletch's face, he would have smartened up immediately. She hoped her partner remembered they were duty bound as police officers to resist their impulses. Apparently, he did, although his voice sounded barely controlled when he spoke.

"Mr. Belmont. You probably want to sit down for a bit and think about things before you say anything more."

Ivy hovered behind Fletch's broad back, her whole body quivering.

In two strides, Joey positioned herself beside her partner so Ivy was fully shielded.

Belmont jabbed his finger at them. "I worked hard my whole life to look after this family and now she thinks she can hang around the house doing nothing? I won't have it. I'll kick her out if she doesn't get a job and start paying her way."

It took a bit of convincing but eventually, Belmont settled down and wove his way upstairs to bed. He didn't seem to notice the younger children standing at the entrance of the kitchen, like a silent jury, watching his progress. The older girl was holding two of her younger siblings by the hand. The ruckus had woken the toddler, who was quietly hugging his quilt. Ivy walked over and picked him up quilt and all.

Their stillness and Ivy's quick recovery from her father's tirade, made Joey think this was a common occurrence. Her nerves twitched as she studied the solemn faces. What else was going on in this household?

"Ivy, who looked after the younger kids while you went out to find your father?"

The teen stiffened for an instant, and then replied, "Mrs. White came over. She does that sometimes to help out." Joey wondered if the neighbor would confirm Ivy's story if asked, but with Fletch hanging over her shoulder, now wasn't the time to dig any deeper so Joey changed subject.

"Is it true you quit school?"

The girl shrugged.

Joey dropped her chin and gave Ivy a stern look. It was easy to forget she was a teenager, until you saw her look down at her feet, shuffle and scowl, before finally giving a reluctant answer. "I've missed some classes when Mom had to work." Ivy's eyes flicked over to the stairs, to where her father had retreated. "No big deal."

The message was clear. There were times when Ivy didn't trust her father with her younger siblings. To Joey, that was a big deal but she also wasn't surprised the girl's mother needed to pick up the extra cash while the hours were needed over the holidays. The poor woman was caught between a rock and a hard place. Joey made a mental note to follow up on that—when Fletch wasn't hovering. Verna Belmont cleaned at the Frost farm once a week so she could catch Ivy's mother there for an unofficial talk. Joey looked up the stairs and wanted to throttle Oliver Belmont. After that, Ivy assured them things would be fine now until her mother got home, and with a final scan around the small, tidy bungalow, they left.

When Joey and Fletch reached the sidewalk, they both looked at the shabby house, and then at each other.

Fletch shook his head, his frown deepening. "I don't like leaving those kids with him. They'd be safer if we took him in," he said.

The situation in the house had Joey's nerves vibrating with so much tension, her muscles ached. "Sure, Fletch. Lock him up. Do you think those kids will thank you for throwing their father in jail? For leaving them alone for Christmas? And will a conviction make it any easier for him to get a job later?"

Fletch strode to the driver's side without another word, leaving her to cross to the passenger seat. Joey glared at him, but didn't have the energy left to butt heads about it. Besides they weren't *real* partners, so it wasn't like they should take turns— he was the boss.

They both slammed their doors with more force than required and snapped their seatbelts on. Fletch turned ice cold eyes on her. He took a deep breath, as if she was wearing on his last nerve. "Belmont needs to take responsibility for his family and for his actions. You're letting him get away with flouting the law, Joey. There has to be consequences. It's not your job to decide when to enforce the law. You can't make it up as you go along."

Joey's control snapped as her mouth opened. "Fletch, I can't mindlessly follow orders. I prefer to think for myself."

Even as the last word escaped through her lips, she wanted to bite off her tongue. She quickly turned away. She was surprised Fletch didn't reprimand her. She shouldn't be mouthing off to a supervisor at any time, but it reflected really badly on her to lose her cool as soon as she came under a bit of stress on the job. Of course, it wasn't the job, and maybe he knew it. That was embarrassing. She was letting Fletch get to her and it had to stop.

She peeked over at him without turning her head. He was staring at the road ahead, frowning at something only he could see, his features flat. Whatever it was, laced the air around them with the suffocating weight of sorrow and loss.

She released her seatbelt and angled toward him. "Fletch. Are you okay?" she asked, at the same time wondering to herself why she cared so much.

The seconds ticked by. Growing up in a house full of men, she knew it was best to stay silent when a guy was upset, so she waited.

When he finally turned toward her, shadows played in his eyes, making them unreadable. "This job is harder than it looks, isn't it?"

The tension between them gradually eased.

"You probably didn't have to deal with kids as a military cop. They make things much harder," she said, softly.

A muscle in his jaw twitched.

They sat that way, in silence, for another moment before Fletch released a heavy sigh.

This is ridiculous, she decided. We can't work like this every day or we'll both go crazy. So he's uptight about procedure and I like to be more flexible? We'll adjust in time. Sure, he got the job she wanted but he didn't know that. They were professionals so it was time she got her head back in the game.

By the time they reached the station a short while later, Fletch had shaken off his mood so she decided not to waste any time. "Come on. Let's go over to Kate's for some real coffee. We need to sort out our relationship."

Fletch stared at her, eyes wide, eyebrows raised. "That's moving fast, isn't it...not that I'm complaining."

"That's not what I meant," Joey said, waving her hand as if erasing her poor choice of words.

Chapter Four

Fletch knew what she meant before she corrected herself quickly, saying, "I meant our working relationship."

With so much conflict in their partnership, what chance would they have in a personal relationship? *Maybe it's a good thing I only committed to three months here in case things didn't work out with Joey*, Fletch thought.

Looking at her now as the flush of embarrassment faded, she looked as drained as he felt. The last call had been hard on both of them. He pulled the moist mountain air deep into his lungs to replace the toxic air from the Belmont house. He'd seen too many suffering children that he couldn't help in war zones. There should be something he could do here.

After watching Joey deal with the Belmont family, there was no doubt in his mind she cared as much as he did. Didn't she realize the laws were in place to help these cases? Didn't she realize she was working against that safety net? What made her think she had the authority to make up her own rules?

The Christmas music playing in the square irritated him as they wove their way through the holiday shoppers. He understood now why Joey was so hot tempered. It wasn't good for morale to bring in an outsider without explanation when there were viable candidates already within the ranks. But why hadn't Rufus told them he'd only taken the job for three months? It wasn't Fletch's place to question his superior but he didn't have to like it. Especially when it put him at odds with Joey.

She was a few steps ahead of him, her long stride eating up the sidewalk. She didn't wait for him at the crosswalk. She stepped into the street. A tan '78 Buick cruised by her so closely, it narrowly missed her toes. Muck splashed over her uniform pants, with some spray reaching as high as her cheeks. She stood with her mouth hanging open as the car continued until it came to a halt at the edge of the curb in front of the Cross Pharmacy.

Now that his split second of panic, when he thought the car might hit her, had passed, Fletch struggled not to laugh. Joey wiped off the mess, muttering things he didn't want to hear as her supervisor. He hung back so he could watch how she handled this incident, hoping she might be more inclined to enforce the law when it smacked her in the face—with dirty slush.

The door of the offending vehicle swung open as Joey bellowed, "Mr. Ingram!" She strode up to the car and stood, arms crossed, as the driver slid forward on the seat, gripped the door firmly and slowly hauled himself upright. He was encased in an oversized puffy down coat, had a woolen hat pulled down over his ears, and a scarf wrapped around his neck and covering his mouth. His unsteady stance made Fletch wonder if they were dealing with a DUI. What was it with these country folk drinking so early in the day? The puzzle was solved when the man turned to face them and Fletch heard the well-worn, raspy voice.

"Hello, Officer Joey. What are you doing out on such a cold morning?" The elderly Mr. Ingram had, at least, eight hard-lived decades on this earth, judging by his worn, leathery skin and faded gray eyes.

When she answered the old man, Joey's temper had been replaced with solicitude. "Don't you remember our talk, Mr. Ingram? You aren't supposed to be driving."

Ingram furrowed his brow. "I have to pick up Mrs. Ingram's medication. You know how bad she feels if she doesn't get it right on time."

Joey shook her head, but kept her voice gentle, "You don't need to do that anymore, Mr. Ingram. Remember? We made special arrangements to have the prescriptions dropped off so you wouldn't have to go out in this cold weather. It's so slippery. You don't want to risk a fall."

Fletch wasn't sure what the hell was going on. He felt for the old guy, but he clearly wasn't competent to drive. Why wasn't Joey taking his license away?

"I guess I got a little confused, Officer Joey."

Fletch saw Joey slip the keys out of his hand as she took his elbow and guided him around the front of the Buick. "Why don't you pop into the station and ask Erik to give you a ride home. We'll drop the car off at your house later on." She helped him step over the snowdrift at the curb, made sure he had his footing on the sidewalk before letting go of his arm, and then watched him enter the station.

When she turned to him, Fletch wasn't sure whether to laugh or bury his head in his hands. Now the police were also a taxi service. "Aren't you forgetting something, Officer Joey?"

She stared at him, her brows knitted together. She had no idea what he was referring to. "The guy nearly ran you over, Joey. Shouldn't you, at least, have asked to see his license and registration? Are you even sure he has a valid license?"

Her eyes rolled upward for an instant. "Of course, he has a license."

"Which you should suspend because he's not a competent driver." Fletch felt like he was talking to a rookie. He had to wonder if Rufus knew about her soft approach to law enforcement because it was really starting to irritate him. Was this why she'd been passed over for the promotion?

She swung the car keys on her finger. "Taking these is faster. Believe me. You really need to review the statutes for suspending a senior's license." Then her voice softened. "Mrs. Ingram took ill a couple of months ago and she isn't going to recover. Before that, he was completely in control of his faculties. This is his last Christmas with his wife of over sixty years, Fletch. I can get all the paperwork going for the whole DMV thing after the holidays. In the meantime, I made him promise not to drive."

She walked away as if the matter was settled. When he didn't follow, she turned. "Aren't you coming?"

It was possible things had changed since he'd lived stateside. It was hard to imagine they'd take *failure to yield to a pedestrian on a crosswalk* off the list of moving violations. Maybe he should review the Vermont Statutes. He shook his head and caught up with her. He desperately needed that coffee.

Kate's Kitchen wasn't what he'd expected to find in a small rural town like Carol Falls. It had the typical wooden tables and chairs, but its décor was international. There were painted bookcases along two walls displaying a couple of globes and a variety of handicrafts, some of which he recognized as Middle Eastern from his tours over there. Maps and photos from different countries covered the walls. Some of the latter showed a tall, auburn haired woman with tribal leaders or foreign politicians. Joey identified her as the Kate in Kate's Kitchen, reminding him she was Officer Wedge's older sister. If she was on site, she must have been in the kitchen because he didn't see her.

It was a busy joint so they decided to get their coffees to go. They wouldn't be able to talk with half the town eavesdropping anyway. He'd have to find another, more private opportunity. While they waited, the customers didn't try to hide their curiosity about his presence. It wasn't clear if they knew who he was or not, although it being a small town, they probably knew what size briefs he wore by now. When the coffees appeared, he reached for his wallet, but Joey beat him to it.

He had time to give that more thought when he was at his desk once more. Things sure had changed since he'd left Carol Falls. There were signs of growth and development that hadn't been here ten years ago, although he was glad the heritage buildings along the main square hadn't been bulldozed in the name of progress. He was certainly surprised at the change in Joey. He could have adjusted to her being a cop but, at this point, he was so thrown by the loose way she treated the law, for a second, he'd actually felt relieved that she meant to pay for her coffee.

Fletch rolled his pen between his fingers. In the military, he was used to trusting his life to the men and women in his unit. It was no problem because everyone followed their orders and stuck to the agreed procedures. Joey was from a different world where she was used to making up her own rules. Maybe her family had enough influence in this town to bend the rules to fit their needs, but surely she'd learned differently in the police academy. They would have taught her that she had a duty to enforce the laws as a police officer or there were serious consequences.

He didn't hear a call come in. It was Joey's sudden movement that snapped him back to attention. He rose from his desk and followed his new partner before she tried to leave him behind again. As they grabbed their jackets he asked, "What's up this time?"

She didn't look happy. "Our town's founder has grown a mustache and council is not impressed."

They'd reached the sidewalk before he decoded her response. "Vandal Gogh has struck again?"

"Yup. A new 'stache on a prominent statue in front of the town hall. The mayor is throwing a fit because there's a council meeting this evening." A tight smile played across her lips, then slipped away. "—and the statue is of his paternal great grandfather, Samuel E. Lincoln the first."

The town hall was across the street from the police station, which made summoning the chief of police to council meetings more convenient for the politicians. Within five minutes Joey and Fletch were shepherded into the mayor's office like two unruly students called before the school principal.

With his tall, fit physique, white blonde hair and deep blue eyes, Mayor Emerson Lincoln had the picture of a perfectly polished politician. They had to listen to a rant about the rising crime in town and the need for a crackdown by the police, before there was an appropriate break for Fletch to say, "Our investigation is progressing well, sir. We are confident we can put an end to the vandalism."

He felt Joey stiffen next to him. Could be she didn't like him speaking about her case but he didn't think so. Something was up with her on this one.

"Well, see to it I'm informed as soon as the culprit is apprehended."

"I'm sure Chief Slayton will be in touch, sir."

She was unusually quiet when they left the mayor's inner sanctum. At the entrance, Fletch reached over her head and pushed open the heavy oak door. He was mildly surprised she didn't comment, although it had been a reflex on his part and not meant to antagonize.

Fletch decided it was time to prod Joey into talking to him. "Let's walk."

As they headed toward the Village Green, he asked, "Have you questioned all the juvies in the vicinity? Are any of the nearby towns reporting similar incidents?"

Joey jolted like he'd popped a balloon in her ear. "Do you think I'm totally incompetent?"

"No. But you must think I am, if you expect me to believe that, given how well you know this town and all the citizens, you don't have a good idea who's behind this vandalism."

She was quiet for a good minute. She didn't look happy about it, but finally admitted, "I *do* know who we're looking for," she said, her voice clipped and tense. "I couldn't be certain this morning, but this latest incident clinches it."

"Great, let's go get him."

Her lips twisted in disgust.

Now what? His frustration in dealing with her was making his muscles twitch. Was the obstacle another person Joey didn't think should be held responsible for the crime? Could it be a Frost? He'd been away a long time so he really knew very little about her extended family.

"Look," he said between his teeth. "I didn't know you wanted the job or that you'd joined the police service. And if I'd known it was so important to you, I would *not* have taken the position. But I didn't know. So, princess, I'm here. I signed the papers. I'm your new deputy. Deal with it."

Her head snapped around and she stopped walking. When she faced him, her expression was mutinous, lips pulled into a thin line, eyes narrowed.

Something about her eyes had changed since their youth. From the first time he'd looked into her warm, intelligent eyes, he'd felt their pull. Had wanted her to share whatever secret thoughts she had hidden in their depths. Now, the trust that had been her lure as a teenager was gone, and a curtain had been drawn to shut him out. Knowing stubborn was her middle name, he tried a calmer approach.

"Who is it, Joey? All we have to do is make sure we put a stop to the vandalism. I'm sure Rufus is a veteran at smoothing things with Lincoln to avoid charges." But it would tick him off if there were two levels of justice, one for the Frosts and one for ordinary people.

He expected her to cross her arms and refuse to talk, but she heaved a sigh. "You've seen what the mayor is like?"

"A pompous ass." At least they could agree on that.

Her face relaxed and a smile slid across her lips. He fought the urge to lean over and kiss them.

"He has a teenaged son."

All thoughts of kissing, and any other pleasurable activity, disappeared. "Don't tell me—"

She nodded and started to walk again. "His one and only son. Sammy. You met him earlier when we went to pick up Belmont."

"How can you be sure it's Sammy?" Wishing his first case in this town wasn't going to get that messy.

She lengthened her stride and couldn't keep her hands still. It was like he'd given her an adrenalin shot.

"On the first two incidents, I went through the usual investigative procedures. It was around the time of the third incident that I remembered a talk we'd heard on vandalism at the academy about the profile of a typical vandal, their characteristics, that sort of thing. I dug out the research." She stopped to take a breath, or maybe to make sure he was following her. He nodded, encouraging her to continue.

"Anyway, the profile is a young teenage boy. And, as I read about the motivations, I realized

Vandal Gogh's targets had a pattern."

Fletch had reviewed the file and hadn't seen a pattern. If she was right about this, he was going to be really impressed. He was also enjoying the way her mind worked.

"All the targets were directly related to Mayor Lincoln."

"He's a political figure. Politicians are always targets of one sort or another."

"No, I mean, *specifically* targeting him. As a person. It wasn't obvious at first, like the statue today. It's *just* a statue outside the town hall, until you consider who the subject of the statue is."

"That could be a coincidence. I read the file. The first incident was *just* a broken window."

"In the mayor's office," she countered.

"It's a stretch," he said, thinking at the same time that she could also be on to something others missed. "What about the second incident, car keying in the parking lot?"

"It was Lincoln's personal vehicle. He was working late that night and his was the only car in the lot. It was assumed others would have been hit, if they'd been parked there. I don't think any others would have been touched."

"What about the third?" Her theory was a stretch, he thought, but that didn't mean her instinct was wrong.

"It was graffiti painted on the side of a vacant building off Main Street."

He tried to picture what had been in the file. "I saw the photo of the mural before it was painted over. It was the typical style, abstract, although the letters on it didn't even make sense. No one could see any political message at all."

There was a gleam in Joey's eye. "That one was brilliant. The letters were a distraction. You've seen those graphic designs that look like completely different images depending on what elements you focus on?"

"Like the one of the old lady that others see as a young woman?"

"Exactly. If you look at the letters as background instead of looking for meaning in them, you can recognize the rear end of a horse—"

"—come on. You can't assume he meant the mayor because of *that*." Tension made his laugh sound sharp.

She didn't smile. "You can when the other end is a caricature of Lincoln's face."

That sobered him up instantly. "Seriously?"

She nodded. "Seriously. And now a moustache on the relative who led the family line into politics? I think Sammy is fed up with it all and no one is listening to him. Which is a classic motivation for this type of vandalism."

Their eyes locked while he thought about it. Then he came to the same conclusion she had. "Damn."

Fletch scrubbed his face with his hands. When had Carol Falls turned into Wisteria Lane? "We have to tell Rufus...and the mayor, before we—"

A woman came up behind them suddenly so they each stepped to opposite edges of the cleared sidewalk to make way for her, and waited for the shopper to power walk between them, filling the full width of the walk with her packages. Joey chuckled as she stepped onto the sidewalk. "Only two more shopping days 'til Christmas—"

Her feet slipped out from under her. Her arms pinwheeled as she tried to regain her balance.

Fletch grabbed her hand as it swung by and yanked, with his other arm stretched out to catch her.

Joey smacked up against his chest with both arms pinned. He relaxed his hold and slid his hands down to take hers. He put a small distance between them but didn't let go. "Sorry. Sometimes I don't know my own strength. I wasn't as gentle as I should have been. Did I hurt you?"

She was breathing hard, eyes wide with shock, but shook her head. They both looked down at their joined hands and let go.

They continued their walk. They stopped at the intersection of Spruce and Main, waited for the light to change, then crossed and started along the nearest path through the Village Green. The air turned cold around them as they reached the red covered bridge at the north end of the park, and were cut off from the warmth of the sun. Fletch broke their silence, working to keep his voice level and his words logical. "Joey, you need to accept that Rufus and the mayor need to know about the boy."

She shook her head with such conviction her woolen hat almost fell off. She yanked it over her ears. "Telling the mayor about this is a really bad idea. Fletch, please trust me on this."

He sucked in a deep breath to ease his frustration with her. "Sweetheart, the boy's parent needs to know his kid's troubled. It's not your job to make decisions for them."

Temper smoldered in her eyes. "There is no way this can end well if we tell either the chief or

Lincoln."

Fletch took a moment to consider the political quagmire they were in. The right thing to do would be to talk to the parent...under normal circumstances. But when the parent is your boss's boss, the holder of the purse strings . . .

"You don't know Sammy, but I do." Joey's voice quivered with intensity. "He's not a trouble maker or delinquent. He's quiet, thoughtful and really smart. But not at all interested in politics. Sammy freezes up every time his father introduces him as *the next mayor of Carol Falls*, which Lincoln does at every event in town. Sammy wants to live his own life instead being pushed into the family business."

She'd said all of this in one breath and now she was holding it. She didn't move, yet every part of her body pleaded with him to do as she asked. She was so close to him, he could smell her shampoo, something flowery, natural and wild. Just like her. He wanted desperately to give her anything she wanted, but they both swore to uphold the law. They both had to keep a firm line between work and personal life. They both had to do the right thing for the boy.

"What if we run it by Rufus and see what he thinks is best." He felt like a coward, but wasn't this what a chain of command was for? If you didn't have the answer, you sent it up the line until you hit the level with enough authority to make a decision. At least that's how they'd done it in the military. Why did this feel more complicated?

Joey gave him the answer when she shook her head firmly, and said, "We can't. He's an elected official, Fletch. You have to give him plausible deniability or you put him in the position of having to tell his boss, the mayor."

Fletch searched her face trying to figure out why it mattered so much to her. He hadn't agreed with her handling of the earlier incidents, but she could probably argue her position. Why was this one affecting her judgement?

Frost Farm was a family business, too, and he'd seen how it had caused tension between the Frost brothers as teens—the heir to the family business was believed to be the favored son. The military was the Fletcher family's business, and he was the only son, the only child. Because of his father's military career, Fletch had traveled the world, learned to be self-sufficient, to trust his own judgement. He'd also paid a price for it. He'd never lived anywhere long enough to call it home. He'd learned early to avoid attachments to people and places so that leaving, when his father was reassigned, was less painful. What had his independence cost him? He would never know for sure.

He shook free of those thoughts, when she grabbed his hand and begged, "Fletch, *please* give me time to talk to Sammy before you tell his father."

It was hard to refuse someone he cared so much about and, at the moment, he wasn't even sure what *was* the right thing to do.

Chapter Five

Joey wanted to shake him. She wasn't asking to let a serial killer slide. Fletch was being stubborn and inflexible—again—and she didn't know how to make him understand.

"Please Fletch. He's just a kid. A good kid. If I can find Sammy, I know I can convince him to tell his father himself. Let me see if I can catch him around town today. It's only a few more hours. If I still can't find him by tomorrow, we can talk to the chief together."

She scanned his face for some sign of conceding, concentrating so intensely she forgot her own tangled emotions. In that moment, she looked past the superficial changes in his features. Something deep inside her heart sparked to life. It sputtered and grew until she knew it was more than the remnants of a teenage romance. From the moment she recognized Fletch as the stranger in the storm, she'd been irritable and moody. Furious that he didn't tell her they'd be working together at the police department. Hurt that he took her promotion away from her. Indignant that he was now in a position to interfere with the job she loved. And, most of all, fearful that she still felt the pull of their chemistry, even when she didn't want to.

If she pushed their mutual antagonism aside for a moment, the past and present intertwined. She found herself looking at a mature and beautiful man. His irritating lack of flexibility now, was the reliability she had loved in her teens. All the girls in school had fallen for the hot football player, but she had seen the strong, disciplined guy who worked for her father and was a good friend to her troubled brother. Even at sixteen, she'd known Fletch was a guy you could always count on. He was a guy you could always trust. Except at the very end. Except with her.

A bubble of emotion swirled in her belly and burst into a flood of heat through her chest. She dropped his hand and turned away from him, in case her face gave away her feelings. Feelings that felt raw and made no sense whatsoever. Joey shrank into her parka to hide her shivering and started to walk again. Now wasn't the time to sort through those emotions. Not with Fletch standing right there.

He must have picked up on something because he strode up and touched her arm to stop her from leaving. "Okay Jo. But we're talking about a *delay*." He turned to leave but stopped, and looked at her as if he had more to say. She waited, afraid that, already, he'd changed his mind. He simply frowned and shook his head. "I hope you do find the boy, but you can't get so emotionally involved in every case, sweetheart, or this job will destroy you."

This time when he turned away, he left, mumbling, "I don't remember it being this damn cold here at Christmas."

Only since you left. He'd surprised her again. Maybe she wasn't the only one with unresolved feelings about the past? She sighed heavily and rubbed her temples. She needed some time alone to think. To remember.

She stuck her hands in her pockets and turned in the opposite direction.

In the fading light, the town's Christmas tree didn't look like much, but in another hour, when it was fully dark, it would be lit up like a galaxy of stars. Every year, the whole town came out to watch the first lighting of the huge Balsam fir tree in the Village Green. She'd been working this year, but swung by on patrol to enjoy the moment and give her brother, Jimmy, a hug when she heard he'd arrived in town.

For most people, the lighting of the tree started the countdown for shopping. Where had the time gone? Only two more days left. She was usually a last minute shopper, but was more on top of things this year. She'd picked up family presents while she was in Burlington a few weeks earlier for a course on Emergency Animal Sheltering.

Uh oh. There was another 'Fletch' issue to deal with. She always gave everyone in the station a little token gift as well. She had something for Wedge, the chief, Taylor. But she didn't know about Fletch then. She couldn't leave him out. But she felt awkward giving him a gift when their...partnership...was so...well, awkward. And since he'd arrived so close to Christmas, would he even think of picking up gifts for the station? Or her?

Strolling toward the community skating rink,

she heard the festive refrain from *The Holly and The Ivy* piped over the loudspeakers—a carol that held so many childhood memories it made her breath hitch. There was one Christmas Eve she'd ended up in tears when her brothers were particularly obnoxious. Her mother told her about a custom in the olden days when the carol was used to resolve squabbles between the townsmen and women. According to tradition, men sang praising holly for its masculine qualities, while the women sang praising the ivy for its feminine qualities. The resolution between the two was with a kiss under the mistletoe. Joey and her mother had giggled at the thought of her brothers having to sing to make up for fighting with her.

Obviously, man problems dated back centuries...and the chance to resolve hers with Fletch under mistletoe brought a tingle to her lips.

She considered sitting on one of several nearby benches. On second thought, if she tried it today, they'd be chiseling her butt off the wooden seat. She watched a couple of kids race up and down the slick ice, only stopping to slap the hockey puck into an imaginary net at each end. The regular floodlights had been swapped out with red and green, and posts were festooned with tinsel streamers and twinkle lights. Joey, like every kid in town, had spent a lot of time hanging around the rink learning to skate or cheering for her favorite guy in a pickup hockey game. It hadn't changed much over the years.

The memory was crystal clear, as if it had happened yesterday instead of a decade ago.

It was a Sunday night. March was going out with a roar, so snow was piled high around the community skating rink. After being cooped up indoors for two days, there was a party atmosphere once the spring storm ended and everyone gathered in the Lincoln Village Green as the rink was cleared. She'd come with her girlfriends, but her brother Jimmy had been given strict instructions to make sure she got home safely.

Skating under the stars had been magical. There were thermoses full of hot chocolate, laughter, songs. Gradually the evening ended and Joey had looked around for her brother. He was nowhere to be found. Fletch was sitting on the bench where she was supposed to meet Jimmy. He was tall and lean, so handsome dressed in a jet-black ski jacket with red stripe details, a red scarf, black wool hat and leather gloves. He wore his dark hair longer then, and it waved near his collar. It was the first time she'd felt his eyes completely on her, scanning her from head to toe and tracking back to stop on her face...as if he was memorizing it.

"Are you ready to go home, Jo?" he'd said, his voice low and seductive.

"Where's Jimmy?" She'd seen him with April Rochester earlier but hadn't noticed him in the last few hours.

Worry crossed Fletch's face, but his response was neutral. "He asked me to make sure you got home safely."

Her body flushed with heat when he stood and took her skatcs from her. He transferred them to his other side, easily holding hers with his own, and then he held out his free hand to her. "Coming?"

Her pulse jumped, her heart raced. The snow, the ice, the lights...everything glowed around her, surreal...dreamlike...as she took his hand and they strolled out of the park together.

At first, it had been awkward, but after a while they'd both relaxed on the walk back to the farmhouse. He told her what it was like to move every time his father was reassigned. At that point, he had never stayed anywhere more than a year or two.

With sudden insight, Joey realized he'd practically warned her off that night on the way home. He said he couldn't let anyone get too close because he always had to leave. She hadn't listened. When they reached the door of the Frost farm, Fletch had let go of her hand and stood facing her. He was a head taller than she at that time, and as he looked down at her, she hadn't understood his expression. Her heart was full of excitement, but he'd seemed sad, like a kid looking through the window of a candy store.

She'd thanked him for walking her home and had put out her hand to take her skates, but instead of giving them to her, he pulled her into his chest and kissed her. On the mouth. At first, it felt like a kiss-and-run, hard but passionate, but then it changed. His mouth softened, his hand cupped her cheek and her world spun out from under her feet. He released her, stepped back, and put her skates in her hand. Then he leaned down to brush her lips with his one more time...and whispered, "Sweet dreams, Jo."

One kiss. Ten years ago. And it still made her mouth water and her heart hurt. Was that because of the kiss? Or because he never spoke to her again after that night. He'd ignored her the last month of school, and then left with his family. Exactly as he'd warned he would. Without saying good-bye. Joey brushed the damp from her cheek. It was senseless to cry over something that happened way back in high school. Even at that age, she'd thought it was stupid to cry over anything—her brothers certainly didn't cry. It was easier to let pride carry her through, and forget it ever happened. Now she was paying the price because it still hurt like hell to think about it.

She pushed the memory into a protected place deep in her heart and headed out of the park. Thinking about the past only made her feel worse, and it wasn't helping her find any answers. Getting back to the investigation would.

Chapter Six

She managed to avoid Fletch when she slipped into the station to pick up the keys to the marked vehicle...and her new canine friend. She figured she'd check out the school and then finally stop at the vet clinic with Buddy. She hoped the dog might bring her good luck and perhaps help her find Sammy Lincoln if he was somewhere off the beaten track. She was prepared to cover as much ground as possible, on foot if necessary, short of knocking on the door of the Lincoln mansion on Maple Farm Road. She was afraid that might make the situation worse.

Buddy was excited to be going for a ride so she'd obviously been in a car with her former owner, whoever that'd been. Taylor had notified Animal Control, the Humane Society and several of the dog rescue groups in the vicinity, to let them know she'd been found, but there'd been no inquiries. Usually, if a pet is wanted and loved, it doesn't take long for someone to come looking when they go missing. If Buddy wasn't loved where she'd been, she *had* become a much loved fixture as station mascot after only a few days. They may have to draw straws for who got to take her home if she was unclaimed.

Joey struck out on finding Sammy in the Village Green, and spent another hour wandering through every nook and cranny in town, before she was ready to admit defeat. She turned off Cedar Road, rounded the traffic circle and eased off the pedal for the drive down Main. On impulse, she swung the wheel to pull into the parking lot of the White Pine High School. The building was closed for the holidays, but it was never locked, and it was warm and dry. Not every teen's choice place to hang, but worth a look.

The building formed a U-shape. The short arm housed the auditorium and the library, while the wing running down the left side was the high school, and the right had the elementary and middle grades. She yanked open the front entrance door to the school and wiped her boots on the industrial mat. She unzipped her coat, but the heat was turned low when classes were out, so she didn't take it off.

After Sammy got too old for a babysitter, he would stop by the Frost farm if he needed help when he was home alone, or wanted company. In elementary school, Sammy had come to the farm once covered in dirt. He'd finally admitted he was being bullied at school. His shy nature, and the fact his father was the town mayor, made him a target. Joey was ready to beat the crap out of the culprits but he refused to let her interfere. She hated bullies and knew, now, she should have stepped in despite her promise not to, although it would have been better if Sammy's father had been able to see what was happening to his son. In Joey's opinion, the mayor had the emotional depth of a puddle and was too caught up in politics to spend time with his son. His mother wasn't the type to intervene.

Just like now. Whatever was going on in Sammy's life, like the teasing at school, the teen would put up with it. Stoic. That was Sammy. Until recently, that is. What could have changed?

As she walked down the empty hall, her footsteps, weighted with her winter boots, echoed loudly through the empty hall. The air in the school was stale, as if it had been closed up much longer than a few days. This was probably a wild goose chase. Why would any kid come back to school when they could be out on vacation? Well, at least she could say she'd done everything she could to warn him things were about to crash down around him.

A door closed around the corner, sounding like the crack of thunder in the oppressive silence.

Joey tensed. "Hello?" she called.

Heels echoed in the distance. A female voice responded. "I'm coming. Who's there?"

She knew the voice of Mrs. Hoadley, an ageless woman, who had reigned over every class of ninth grade students for twenty-five years.

"It's me, Mrs. Hoadley. Joey Frost." She relaxed and waited for the woman to appear.

The older woman charged around the corner at the far end of the hall with powerful strides and collided into Joey with a bear hug. "Hello, dear. I meant to call you about coming in for Career Day. Will you still do your talk this spring?"

"Absolutely. I wouldn't miss it," Joey answered, returning the embrace of the woman who had encouraged her to find her passion and make it her career. She'd never forgotten that advice. Or the woman who gave it to her. Although it had taken her a few years to summon the courage to heed it.

"I was wondering if you'd seen Sammy Lincoln today." Seeing a flash of concern in the teacher's eyes, Joey tried to deflect it by adding, "You know he lives near my parents?"

"Oh, yes. I'd forgotten. You just missed him."

Joey hadn't really expected to hear she'd almost found him. "I didn't think you gave detention during the holidays, Mrs. Hoadley," she quipped, hoping to find out the real reason Sammy was there.

The teacher chuckled. "Some of the kids deserve it, but not Sammy. He's such a sweet boy. He's been tutoring little Ivy Belmont. She's hardly been at school at all these last few months." Her face sagged suddenly, revealing the ravages of age that were usually hidden by her vitality. "So sad, that whole situation. I have a mind to give Ollie Belmont a piece of my mind—letting drink get in the way of caring for his family."

"Christmas is an emotional time," Joey said. "I'm sure he'll pull it together once the pressure is off in the new year." She hoped she sounded more confident than she felt. It had already been a year since council budget cuts had cost him his job with the town. Since then, Garret had tried to give him a chance at the Frost farm, but was forced to let him go for drinking on the job.

Her former teacher seemed more optimistic. "I think Sammy and Ivy are hoping so. That's why they're trying so hard to keep up with her school work. Those two are such a cute young couple and so good for each other."

Joey hid her surprise. She'd thought they were friends. Sixteen seemed so young to her now. "Sammy didn't mention he and Ivy are dating."

"It started in the fall. At least, that's when I noticed them cuddling in the library—they've both always retreated into books, you know, since they were kids. But it was this September that I noticed their friendship had blossomed into romance. They suddenly radiated that depth of emotion only possible between sixteen year olds." Mrs. Hoadley's vision drifted briefly with her own warm memories.

Joey absolutely could remember the twisting pain that burrowed a hole in your chest when that first big romance went south. She set her mind back on the job.

"Do you know where they were headed, Mrs. Hoadley?"

"They popped their heads into the library and said they were heading home but, well, you know kids. They may have changed directions as soon as they were out the door." She shrugged. "I wish I could be more help."

"You have been, Mrs. Hoadley, more than you know," Joey said, giving her mentor a hug and repeating her promise to arrange her annual talk to the graduating class.

The older woman returned the way she'd come.

Joey could feel the case falling into place. Young love. That was the final piece. The Carol Falls crime wave was triggered when two troubled families intersected. She should have picked up on it outside Billy Boy's Bar, but she was so distracted by Fletch's presence she'd missed it. She hadn't clued in to why the kids were standing there together, trying to bring her father home. Sammy had said his father made bad decisions. Was he blaming his father for Belmont's job loss? Why not? Oliver Belmont was telling anyone who'd listen, including his impressionable daughter. Why wouldn't she believe him and then tell her boyfriend? Joey finally had what she'd been looking for in the vandalism case. With the two fathers acting like adolescents, is it any wonder one kid is acting like a little mother, old beyond her years and the other one is acting like a juvenile delinquent, which he isn't. Could this situation get any more screwed up?

Joey looked around the dark gray hall, the dented lockers, and the scuffed hardwood floor of the high school. It seemed so long ago now when she'd started that new stage of her life filled with excitement. It had ended in bruising teenage heartache. She had strolled down the corridor to class, her thoughts filled with the memory of Fletch's kiss the night before. Her heart jumped when she saw him standing at his locker. She'd only had eyes for him, so she didn't notice he was talking to a leggy football groupie. He looked right at her, through her, really, and didn't say anything. He might as well have struck her. Because something inside her broke at that moment.

Chapter Seven

Between Fletch's presence, and the situation with the Belmonts, Joey was beyond exhausted when she pulled into the driveway of her small bungalow on Fir Street that evening. Her parents had always left the front porch light on for her at the farmhouse, but she still hadn't developed the habit in her own home. Worse than that, she'd been so busy all through December, with the course in Burlington the whole first week and then crazy work hours ever since, she still hadn't put up her Christmas lights. How depressing. If you didn't know the pale gray stucco one story was nestled in among Winterberry shrubs, you might think it was an empty, overgrown lot.

Joey dragged her feet through the knee-high snow in her driveway, making a mental note to come out to shovel once she'd had a bite to eat. Living in her own place—having her independence—sounded a whole lot more exciting before she knew the work involved in home ownership. Her job didn't allow for a lot of spare time.

She secured her weapon and badge, and tried to lock away her worries along with them. It was only when she let Buddy out the back door that Joey suddenly remembered she'd meant to stop at the vet on her way home from the school.

"Damnation, Buddy. Couldn't you have barked or something when we left the school to remind me?"

The dog tilted her head and cocked both eyebrows.

"Of course you wouldn't. What am I thinking? It's not like you want to go to the vet."

Soup from a can and a tuna sandwich might not sound like a meal to some, but anything that was quick, easy and hot met the criteria for Joey. It gave her the energy she needed, and an hour later she was pitching shovelfuls of heavy wet snow onto the waist-high pile growing beside her driveway. She had started at the curb and was almost to the garage. Only another couple of feet and she'd be done. She stretched the kinks out of her muscles and then repositioned the edge of the shovel where she'd left off.

"Need a hand with that?"

She hadn't heard Fletch's approach from behind and fought to slow her racing pulse. "You shouldn't sneak up on someone at night. I could have swung around and decked you with my shovel."

He gave her a crooked grin. "Nah, your reflexes are too fast not to recognize me and stop before it connected."

She leaned on the shovel and looked at him with one eyebrow raised. "How do you know I wouldn't have kept swinging anyway?"

His smile didn't waver. "I didn't, but *my* reflexes are fast enough to stop it if you did."

She shrugged. "It's really no fun when we're evenly matched, is it?"

His smile took on a wicked edge. "Oh, it can be. Depends on what we're doing."

She didn't have an answer to that. As teens, they'd never played verbal games, and since they'd reconnected as adults, they'd mostly been at odds.

He held out his hand for the shovel. Pride battled with fatigue for a moment. Fatigue won. After handing it over, she stepped onto the path out of his way and stood watching him. His lightweight ski jacket—she recognized it as high-end technical skiwear—allowed for maximum freedom of movement, and showed the economical tension and release of his well honed muscles. He hadn't bothered to zip up, so she could admire the development of his chest, the flat stomach muscles, and the firm thighs wrapped in worn denim jeans as he worked his way to the end of her driveway, not even breaking a sweat.

Watching him, something shifted near her heart, startling her. She crossed her arms, as if by doing so, she could protect it. The athletic boy she'd known had grown into a strong man although he'd kept the efficient, graceful movements he'd perfected in sports. The feelings she'd had for Fletch as a teenager, and had set aside as lost and forgotten, had also grown and matured over time— while she'd been focusing on her career. It was as if fate had brought him to her this time as a challenge to her career and her heart. Could she have both or was she supposed to choose?

Then he rested the shovel against the garage door, walked over to where she stood...and reached for her.

She stepped away.

He pointed to the mistletoe her five year old nephew had insisted on hanging on the garden arch above her head, but shrugged and dropped his arms to his side without comment. He turned to look at the mountains in the distance.

"You were my best friend's sister, Jo. In the teenage guy world, that means hands off. But I should have said a proper good-bye. I'm sorry I didn't."

The muscles in her throat cramped with the effort of holding in her tears. They were both adults now and he was back, so why did any of it matter anymore? She ignored the little voice whispering that, perhaps, it was because she was feeling all those intense, confusing emotions, the stabbing pain, in her heart—again. "It was years ago. I was being childish and stupid to even bring it up—"

He turned his laser gaze on her and laughed. "Joey Frost, even when you *were* a kid, you were never childish or stupid."

The warmth in his voice eased her nerves a little. She needed to understand it, to get over a rejection from someone she'd loved and trusted. She couldn't help it. "If kissing me was so bad, why couldn't you pretend it didn't happen? We could've gone back to the way things were, for that last month you were in town. But you snubbed me in school. When we passed in the hall, you turned away. You ignored me."

"I thought the kiss was a mistake, not that it was bad. I couldn't possibly forget kissing you.

When I put my mouth on your lips, that was it for me. I wanted you more than anything I'd ever known in my life."

The unhappiness in his eyes weakened her. "Then why, Fletch? Why hurt me like that?"

"For one thing, your brother saw us on the porch."

"Who? Jimmy? He couldn't have, that was the night he eloped with April. "

"Not Jimmy. Garret."

"Garret? So what?"

Fletch turned away from her and scuffed at the snow with his foot, suddenly reminding her of the teenager she remembered. "He wanted to protect you."

There was more. Something Fletch wasn't telling her. Childish or not, she really wanted to stamp her foot now. "What did he say?"

That crooked grin was there, but his eyes were still sad. "He told me what I needed to hear."

"Which was—?"

"God, you aren't going to let this go, are you?" Fletch said. "He reminded me that he'd heard I'd be leaving town any day. He asked me if I was the kind of guy who'd fool around with his best friend's sister and then move on when my father was reassigned. Had I thought about how much I might hurt you when I left?"

"That's all? And you ran off with your tail between your legs."

This time his smile was full of charm. "Well, he may also have added something about beating the crap out of me if I ever laid hands on you again."

She did not see the humor in it. Anger roared

up, making her ears ring. "He had no right to interfere."

"No, probably not. I wouldn't have listened, except I knew he was right, Jo. I *was* leaving in another month, and it *would* have hurt you when I left. I thought it would be easier on you—on both of us—if I stopped everything before it started and put some distance between us. It'd always worked for me before. I'm not proud of it, but I did what I'd always done. I backed away."

"You did warn me," she said. "That night when you walked me home. But I didn't listen, so I guess I can't hold it over you forever. You were around the house all the time that year, and I guess I believed you always would be, and then suddenly you were gone. I missed you so much."

Fletch stepped closer, and this time she moved in. She didn't realize she was crying until he took off his glove and wiped her cheek. "I'm so sorry, Jo. I missed you. too. I handled it all wrong because I was too young and stupid to handle it properly."

When he pulled her into his arms this time, it felt right. As the weight of the past slipped away, she drew away slightly and smiled at him. "At sixteen, I didn't know how to handle it properly either."

His lips brushed her ear. "I'm not young or stupid anymore, Jo. I promise."

His thumb stroked her cheek, before he let his mouth follow the same path...until it found its true destination. He brushed her lips with a light kiss. Only enough to leave her craving more, then he rested his brow against hers. "Now, do you think we could take this discussion inside before we freeze our tails off?" He eased back, tucked a hand under her chin to lift her face to his. His sly grin was in place. "You could put the coffee on while I finish this up. That is, if you've finished checking out my butt."

"Uh-ah. I wasn't—"

Who was she kidding? Of course, she was. And she got caught. Joey tried for nonchalance. "Sure, do you take cream or sugar with your coffee?"

He finished shoveling and was kicking the snow off his boots in less than two minutes. Now, with Fletch in her home, Joey felt shy all of a sudden. She'd dated in college, but had let the job take over her life ever since. He strolled into her kitchen and leaned on the doorjamb like he belonged there. She flicked a look over her shoulder to make sure he was really there. She kept the coffee maker on the counter, but almost spilled the grounds on the floor as she measured it out, and then knocked the mugs together trying to get them out of the cupboard. Finally he took over, moved her to one side, and got the coffee safely going.

Closing the distance between them, he slid his fingers along her jawline until he circled her neck and tugged her forward. When they were nose to nose, he dropped his head to kiss her lightly, first on one side of her mouth, then the other. He pulled back just enough to look into her eyes, and then settled his mouth firmly on hers.

She reached up to touch his cheek...let her fingers push into his hair. She pulled him closer. His hand was warm on her back and she worried her knees would buckle as he deepened the kiss.

The coffee maker dinged when it was ready, interrupting them. However, once the steaming mugs sat on the coffee table, they were forgotten, until they got cold.

Time slipped away. He'd been gone too long, but it felt as if he'd never left. Joey touched him, afraid she was imagining him there and worried he might disappear again if she blinked. He watched the path of her fingers as she explored his body, trailing over the corded muscles of his strong arms, the solid curve of his chest, the ridged abdomen. His wasn't the kind of body you built in a gym, his muscles were honed from hard labor and harsh conditions. When she found a ragged scar that hadn't been there a decade before, she palmed it gently, but didn't question its origin. Maybe someday he would tell her what his life overseas had been like, but she knew some soldiers never spoke of it.

He linked his fingers with hers and guided them to his mouth, kissing each one. "The past is behind us now, Jo. We can move on from here."

It shocked her, how his presence anchored her. Why did she need someone now to—literally—hold her hand? Amid all the turbulence of the last few days, she was suddenly grounded in a way she hadn't felt before. The feeling shook her senses...her certainty about her life. She'd been fine on her own before Fletch showed up. She had a full life in a town she loved, with family and friends...and a great job. Yet, in truth, her personal life had been incomplete. Lonely.

Oh, but *this* was still a very bad idea. They worked together. He was her superior.

It didn't matter though, because she'd waited so long to be with Fletch, she didn't care. She looked at their joined hands and tightened her grasp.

She had only a moment to change her mind before his lips curved on hers once more and he crushed her against his chest and locked his arms around her. Maybe she was making a huge mistake, but at this moment, she didn't care. She allowed her thoughts to crumble into disjointed fragments until she was left with only sensations and raw feelings. Her teenage daydreams had not come even close the real thing with Fletch. The tight grip she'd held on her heart relaxed and then slipped away.

~~~

The next morning, heavy breathing in her ear roused her from a deep sleep. She'd been dreaming and—

"Fletch?"

A sloppy, wet tongue stroked the back of her hand. Her eyes popped open. She blinked at seeing her bed partner. "Buddy, off!" she commanded, as she pushed the mutt away. The clock glowed seven-thirty in the early morning light seeping through her bedroom blind. Her pulse picked up remembering how she'd spent the evening. She turned on her side and smoothed the pillow with her hand. It was late when Fletch left—they'd both been anxious to avoid gossip if neighbors saw them leaving her house together in the morning—so she was lucky Buddy woke her. She'd forgotten to set her alarm for work.

Despite the lack of sleep, she felt alert, energized and relaxed. She leaned her head against the pillows and ran a finger across her lips, still tender from the night before. Could it have been a dream, like she'd had so many times over the years? She touched her mouth again to reassure herself that, yes, this time, it was real. Fletch had finally come home.

The sensations writhing through her body had certainly been real, more than she'd ever felt before. Joy, need, passion. Every emotion had struck with scorching intensity. The afterglow now was an ache, not painful, but strong, squeezing her heart tight enough to make it difficult to breathe. She'd thought she was in love with him at sixteen. Now, she was *afraid* she was in love with him.

But was this the real thing? What if it was a one-night stand to him? She'd been so dazed by his presence, by the moment, she hadn't thought beyond the next kiss. In the full light of day, it was easier to remember how much her career meant to her. Whether she saw him again outside of work or not, this wasn't going to make their working relationship any easier for sure.

With a shiver, she rubbed her breast bone and headed for the shower.

She was in her SUV when she decided to give her search for Sammy Lincoln one last effort. She wasn't ready for Fletch to tell her she'd run out of time. She didn't expect him to cut her any slack at work because of the change in their personal relationship. And, he'd only promised to *delay* telling the chief she suspected the boy. He hadn't said for how long. She was counting on out-of-sight, out-of-mind while she spent a few more hours looking.

Buddy wheedled her way into the front seat but, despite her vigilant watch, they had no more luck finding the boy. She'd started by taking Buddy for a walk through the park, and then retraced her steps from the day before in case someone had seen Sammy. With the kids out of school and the weather warm and sunny, it shouldn't be this hard to locate one teenager. She considered making up an excuse to call his parents' house, but concluded it would simply bring things to a boil sooner. She might as well get the chief's advice on how to handle the mayor first.

She was almost at the police station when she saw her mother's car parked in front of Kate's Kitchen, so she bypassed the station and pulled in behind.

Sylvia Frost straightened from the back seat, struggling with a baby carrier, a diaper bag and her equally large handbag.

"Need a hand with all that, Mom?" Joey closed the car door for her.

"Hello, Josephine. I haven't seen much of you lately." At fifty-six, Sylvia was a strikingly beautiful woman, confident enough to leave her hair silver, and vain enough to keep it perfectly styled. Joey always felt like an amazon next to her elegant mother, having inherited her height, strong build and coloring from the Frost side of the family.

"I know, Mom, sorry. With the storm and everything I've been putting in extra hours at work." Joey shouldered the diaper bag and took the purse, knowing her mother wasn't going to relinquish the baby.

Sylvia scanned Joey's face as if looking for signs of chicken pox. "By *everything* do you mean the new deputy police chief?"

Heat crawled up Joey's neck to her face, eliminating any need for a verbal answer. Baby Holly wasn't the only topic zipping through the Carol Falls' grapevine. "Mom, I've been meaning to ask you if you've been able to bring Holly in for a full checkup yet." She knew the answer from Wedge's file but it would take her mother's mind off her daughter's love life.

"Oh, yes. I did that right away. Our little angel is perfectly healthy." Her mother stroked the infant's cheek with a gentle hand. Sylvia was in love, for sure. "The Ladies' Auxiliary meeting will be starting in about twenty minutes. I promised I'd come early with Holly so we'd have lots of time for a visit beforehand," Sylvia replied as she fussed with the carrier, making sure the baby was completely protected from the cold.

Joey scooted ahead to yank open the heavy storm door of the cafe so her mother could precede her into the warm interior with the baby. Her mouth watered the instant she followed them inside. The enticing aroma of hot coffee and freshly baked muffins wrapped around her like a blanket. Joey changed her mind about heading right back out the door for work. She quickly retrieved Buddy from outside, settled her with the car blanket and a bowl of water inside the storm door, then pushed through the inner door into the café again to grab a coffee and pick up some goodies for the station.

Kate Wedge, the owner of Kate's Kitchen, was circulating around the room, filling coffee cups and setting out baskets of croissants, bagels, and other oddly-shaped baked goods from around the world. She stopped to ask the Belmonts' neighbor, Mrs. White, about her rheumatism and again to see how Peter Boychuk's wife was doing with her new baby. Despite all her years away as a journalist, Kate had woven herself quickly into the very fabric of Carol Falls again. It was more than her charm. It had to be a skill.

As Joey's mother moved into the crowd, it was obvious this wasn't the baby's first visit with the ladies. There were *oooohs* and *aaaahs* as the women jostled for the privilege of taking the baby out of her restraints, removing her winter clothing, soothing whatever discomfort she was experiencing, and handing her from person to person with appropriate cuddling along the way.

Joey knew the names of all the women in the room. It was odd that the mayor's wife wasn't among them since Mrs. Lincoln was a quiet, but very active, member of the group. A sliver of memory quivered to life in a corner of Joey's mind. There'd been a nasty rumor around town the summer before, that Taylor Pope had lost her job with the mayor at his wife's insistence. Joey didn't recall any mention of an actual affair. True or false, it might explain Taylor's aloofness.

Joey pushed office issues out of her mind and strolled over to the large harvest table in the center of the café, the only one large enough to seat all the ladies attending the meeting. She set the diaper bag and her mother's purse within easy reach, and then silently helped her mother out of her coat. Some of the ladies had little gifts for the infant—a special diaper rash cream made from a secret family recipe, a night light in the shape of a Christmas candle, and a hand sewn bib with pretty red bows appliqued all over it. Baby Holly had become their shared Christmas treasure. Their actions confirmed Joey's instinct that the baby belonged here in Carol Falls. Which meant little Holly was one of Joey's people. She would find a way to reunite that precious infant with her mother.

I may know squat about babies, but I bet I know who's likely to have a good idea where that baby came from, she thought as she scanned the room. With a fresh cup of coffee in hand, she turned to join the gaggle of women—and nearly smacked Verna Belmont in the chin with her mug.

"Oh, Verna, I'm sorry. I didn't realize you were there."

"My fault, Officer Frost." Her voice wavered, and was so soft Joey had to lean forward to catch her words. Oliver Belmont's wife was only a dozen or so years older than Joey, but it might as well have been decades. What you could see of her face was pale and drawn. The poor woman kept her head bowed, and with her fine wisps of fair hair falling forward around her face, it was as if she was hiding within her own body. She was obviously aware of, and probably embarrassed about, their official visit to her home the day before with her husband.

With a small nod, Verna moved past her, pushing a rope mop to clean the wet footprints Joey and her mother had tracked in.

Joey took a seat at a nearby table to eavesdrop on the ladies' pre-meeting chatter while she sipped her coffee. Before long, she was absorbed into the group and a steady stream of information ebbed and flowed around her. She wasn't patient by nature but knew that, here, she would hit the mother lode. Pun intended, she chuckled to herself.

It took the rest of the morning to get what she hoped was all the information they had. According to the townswomen, who between them had birthed more babies than the maternity ward in Montpelier, baby Holly was never in any risk the night she was abandoned. The ladies agreed that it was significant that the baby had been left somewhere that assured her prompt discovery. Someone wanted her in safe hands, no matter if those hands weren't her mamma's. Apparently, whoever gave birth to the infant, or someone with the birth mother, knew how to swaddle the baby properly to keep her warm and comfortable—something the police would never notice or think to ask about.

"How are you, sweetie?" Fletch's Aunt Elle asked Joey, in a voice meant for everyone at the table to hear.

Joey squirmed knowing she was under a microscope but not sure how to escape. She tried to stay calm. "Same old, same old."

"That's not what I hear." The older woman smiled.

Joey bit her lip. Had Fletch been talking to his aunt about her? He couldn't have, they'd only gotten together the night before. She couldn't keep the bitterness out of her tone when she replied, "Seems the boss found money for that deputy chief position he's been wanting once he had Fletch lined up for the job."

Aunt Elle patted her hand and winked at her. Several of the other ladies smiled, as if they had a shared secret. Her mother was no help, pretending she was busy with the baby instead of rescuing her own daughter.

"I know his contract is only three months but don't you worry, sweetie. I don't see him taking that job in Boston. I'm betting he stays right here in Carol Falls. True love has a way of working itself out if it's meant to be."

Joey's heartbeat hitched. She sucked in a deep breath and tried to level herself out. God bless small towns, Joey thought. No one keeps a secret for long. Not even Fletch. He thought he could swing back into town, use her for booty calls while he was here, and then stroll on to his new job without a backward glance. By the time the women wound down and were ready to return to their day-to-day lives, it wasn't caffeine making her heart pump, her nerves twitch, and energy surge through her muscles like a river about to overflow its banks. Hell hath no fury like a woman who's been used. That wasn't one of her grandmother's sayings, but it was going to be one of hers. Time to get back to the station and slam Noel Fletcher for being a scumbag in officer's clothing.

Chapter Eight

Joey stumbled out of Kate's Kitchen with Buddy into the fresh air. She barely had time to glance around to make sure no one was paying attention before she collapsed against the side of the building. Buddy rubbed against her leg in sympathy as she wrapped her arms around her waist and squeezed her eyes shut trying to keep the humiliation locked inside. *Damn that man. I thought his feelings last night were real. I believed last night was our chance to start something together. How could I be so stupid? Fletch still only lives in the moment and then moves on...without a word or a thought for anyone.*

Anger sparked to life under her rib cage, forcing her to suck in a deep breath. She focused on its slow burn, slowing her pulse as she gradually regained control. *No point over reacting to what could turn out to be town gossip. I'm not sixteen anymore. I'm an adult. I can handle a meaningless hook-up and walk away.* She ignored the little voice that added, *Not with Fletch, you can't. I wanted my* independence. To exercise my freedom. He's a great-looking guy. No biggy. A bit of fun. She pushed away from the building and let her arms drop to her side. She squared her shoulders, gave them a shrug to loosen up, and strode to her jeep. For now, she had a job to do.

By the time Joey was settled at her desk, with Buddy stretched out at her feet, she was churning somewhere within that fine line between love and hate. Maybe with time, and more effort, she'd find something closer to nonchalance. For now, she was glad Fletch was in with the chief so she didn't have to deal with either of her bosses.

Her wish didn't last long, however. Ten minutes later, Fletch stuck his head out and signaled her to join them. She could feel the tension vibrating through his body. He waited for her to reach him before he whispered, "Where've you been? Do you set your own hours, too?"

Joey wasn't used to having close supervision and hadn't thought to call in. And, obviously, their evening together hadn't brought any warm fuzzies to their office relationship for him this morning. She noticed his jaw muscles working as she stepped past him into the office. Nodding to the chief, she said, "I was working the Baby Doe file at the cafe with the Ladies Auxiliary." Knowing it would make Fletch the outsider, she added, "Sir, Mrs. Slayton asked me to remind you to pick up milk on your way home."

Chief Slayton nodded but didn't respond with his usual wisecrack. Once she sat down, he asked, "So what did you find out from the ladies this morning?"

Fletch leaned forward, resting his elbows on his thighs and angled his head, ready to listen. That put him too close for Joey's comfort. She took a shallow breath and reminded herself he was leaving in a couple of months. She stiffened her spine and gathered her thoughts to bring her superior up to date.

"Sir, the entire coffee club—"

Fletch frowned. "The who?"

Joey spat the answer without looking at him. "It's the Carol Falls Ladies' Auxiliary."

"Auxiliary to what?" His tone snapped back at her.

Their boss frowned, likely puzzled by the tension sizzling between his two officers, stepped in. "Beats me. The wife goes out about once a month to have coffee with her friends." His voice had the usual affectionate, but slightly mocking tone he used when speaking about the group. "I generally refer to it as her *coffee club*."

That label stuck around the station, Joey included, which made her feel a little sheepish after she'd learned that morning what the group actually did do. "The main purpose of the Ladies' Auxiliary is to support our community and any of the neighboring towns in an emergency. They provide hot coffee and sandwiches to fire fighters while they battle a blaze, or look after displaced citizens during a flood." She glared at each man to emphasize the importance of the women's role. "Anyway, as Chief Slayton said, they meet once a month at Kate's Kitchen."

"So what could they tell you that we didn't know?" The chief wasn't ready to let go of his notion that the group was simply an excuse for a coffee break.

"It's more what they *notice* that we don't. We

looked at everything at the scene as evidence, and figured the birth mother cared enough to ensure the baby would be found quickly. They take in the scene as mothers. They saw that whoever wrapped the baby in that quilt, knew a lot about wrapping babies."

"What's there to know? You put a blanket around 'em."

"That's my point. There's a lot more than sticking a blanket on the kid, apparently. Women have been swaddling their newborns for thousands of years, so they sleep longer and fuss less. Holly was properly swaddled inside her baby quilt when she was found."

The big man leaned forward in his chair. "You mean a doctor or nurse was present at the birth?"

"Possibly, but not necessarily. All the women at Kate's know how to do it because they've had children. So it only tells us the mother, or someone with her, had experience swaddling babies."

The chief heaved a mighty sigh. "That's serious. You can understand an unwed teen panicking and leaving the baby to be found. But if a mature adult was involved—"

Joey agreed. She'd spent an hour or so with baby Holly that morning and was having a much harder time keeping her objectivity now. She also felt an obligation to the coffee club.

"Sir, I hadn't appreciated until this morning how much knowledge and information about our town those women have."

Chief Slayton accepted her perspective with pursed lips. She hoped he'd start showing his wife's group a little more respect. Joey planned to do so from now on.

Finally, when the two men exchanged a look over her head, Joey pushed up from her chair, more than ready to leave. With a wave of his hand, the police chief motioned her back down.

"Before you go, Frost—"

She closed her eyes to keep her very experienced senior officer from reading her like a bathroom magazine. She didn't want him to see there was more going on than a tiff between partners. If he noticed, he didn't comment.

As she reluctantly sank into her chair, Fletch shifted in his. She glanced at him. What's with the rigid posture? Was he regretting their night together, too? He definitely looked uncomfortable.

While she pondered his behavior, he spoke up, but avoided her gaze. "We had another visit from the mayor this morning. A bag of flaming dog sh— uh...excrement, was left on his doorstep at his home."

She snickered, breaking the tension that had drawn her muscles tight as guitar strings, then quickly covered it with a cough. Neither of the men in the room seemed to see the humor. Chief Slayton remained solemn as Fletch informed her in a flat, impersonal voice that, while she was out of the office, he'd been called to the mayor's home to take a statement from Mrs. Lincoln, and had then proceeded to the mayor's office to collect his version of the incident.

"Mayor Lincoln definitely did not appreciate the practical joke."

"I bet not," Joey replied, all her instincts on overdrive. This was leading up to something she wasn't going to like.

Fletch finally turned to her but his striking face

gave away none of his thoughts...or emotions. "So. Was it Oliver Belmont or Sammy Lincoln?"

Fletch's tone was more interrogator, than colleague. Why was he on the offensive? Or mad at her? And why were they asking about Sammy? Joey looked from one man to the other and shook her head. "Sammy'd never risk his mother opening the door first."

"Belmont?" Fletch clamped his lips into a tight line.

"It's consistent with Belmont's vendetta against the mayor," she said. "But from the look on your faces, I'm guessing you don't have enough to pick him up."

Fletch answered. "No witnesses."

"Fletcher tells me you've zeroed in on a suspect for the vandalism. Can you run through that for me?"

The sudden rise in her blood pressure nearly blew out her ear drums. She shot a glare at Fletch. He stared at the floor. How could such a stickler for protocol be so quick to break the unwritten rules about taking someone else's case to the chief? And what about his promise to her about delaying?

Wary now, she didn't turn her back on him, and schooled her features into a neutral expression, to report directly to Chief Slayton. "I'm unaware of what Deputy Chief Fletcher has told you, sir. I've analysed all the incidents in the context of current research and have developed a hypothesis—"

"Cut the crap, Frost." The chief's tone was sharp. "Your instincts about the people in this town are never wrong. If you think it's Sammy Lincoln, then it probably is. And when I called his father, he didn't seem all that surprised."

"You called the mayor?" Joey clenched her teeth to stop any further comment from escaping and sucked in a lungful of air. "I'm not sure what you need me for, sir. It appears you and the deputy chief have the case under control." She looked at the wall just past her superior's head. If she looked directly at him, he might see the glisten of tears in her eyes. "If there's nothing further, I'll transfer the file immediately."

She'd kept the quiver out of her voice, but the strain was taking its toll. She needed to get out of this office. If Fletch so much as spoke to her, she'd break. She managed to hold it together when the chief said, "Joey, let's not be like that. This is a small department and we work together. You weren't here when the complaint came in so Fletcher gave me the briefing. He wasn't trying to undermine you."

She looked at Fletch through narrowed eyes, but she replied more carefully. "Of course, he wouldn't do that, Chief. Naturally, as my superior, Deputy Chief Fletcher had every right to discuss the case with you and act on it any way he sees fit." But she and Fletch knew this wasn't really about him working her case. It was about breaking his promise to keep her speculations to himself while she looked for Sammy. So much for trust between partners. Between lovers.

She forced herself to focus on the investigation and ran through the same reasoning she'd given Fletch, and then moved on to her visit with Sammy's teacher at the high school.

"Even though I could see the common thread linking everything to Sammy and his father, I had no concrete *evidence*." Her tone communicated her low opinion of her partner ignoring the importance of that fact. "Their relationship has been on a downward spiral for years, so I couldn't see what might have triggered Sammy's sudden change in behavior."

"But, you've figured it out now?" her boss asked.

"Mrs. Hoadley from the high school gave me the answer this morning."

Both men cocked their heads in unison, their attention fully on what she was saying. "Sammy Lincoln has been in a romantic relationship with Ivy Belmont since at least this fall. She's been missing a lot of classes because of her father, so Sammy's been helping her keep up with her schoolwork."

Both men leaned back in their chairs.

The chief's voice was laced with resignation when he spoke. "And the two fathers have been working themselves up into a feud since the fall."

"Exactly," Joey said.

Chief Slayton's face seemed to slide down an inch, adding an extra couple of years. "Why didn't I just retire last year when the wife told me to?"

Joey smiled at the man she'd known since childhood. "You'd've been bored."

He chuckled. "Probably." Then shook his head. "Lincoln senior will handle his son and we can close the case. I, for one, am relieved to have this one off our plate. Good job, Officer Frost."

"Thank you, sir." Joey was anxious to get out of the stuffy office...out of the building...and as far from Fletch as she could possibly get.

With another heavy sigh, the chief said, "Get back to work."

Joey rose stiffly from her chair one more time and almost bumped into Fletch. She jerked as if burned. Her heart ached, but she refused to let it interfere with her job. If Fletch was leaving in three months, then she still had a chance at that promotion...if she could close out these cases. Maybe working with Fletch would improve her chances of doing just that. All she had to do was get her emotions under control.

She pushed past Fletch and bolted from the chief's office.

Fletch followed on her heels and caught her as she reached her desk. "Jo, I need to explain."

"No you don't." She picked up the coffee she'd left behind when he'd called her into the office. She dropped her voice so only he would hear her. "I should have known not to trust you. You don't care about Sammy or anyone else in this town. And me, least of all."

Fletch opened his mouth to respond, but the main door at the front of the station swung open and smashed into the wall. Both she and Fletch jumped and faced forward, each with a hand hovering over the butt of their weapon.

Joey seriously considered shooting Mayor Emerson Lincoln where he stood in the entrance, flushed with temper...and completely oblivious to the reaction he had caused inside the patrol room. As she breathed in and dropped her hand away from her hip, she glanced around and saw Fletch do the same. Wedge, rigid in an identical position, had jumped up so fast from his desk that his chair was over on its side. Taylor had kicked her chair backward to take cover behind a support pillar in her alcove, her face the color of wax paper. At the door of his office stood Chief Slayton, and there was no doubt he was also giving serious thought to an illegal use of his firearm.

"Are you all right?" Fletch leaned close to whisper in her ear.

Joey looked down at the coffee still in her left hand, glad she hadn't yet popped off the lid. "He didn't make me drop my coffee," she whispered back.

"Or you would have shot him?"

"Darn right." She hoped she'd made it sound light, but it shook her that he could read her thoughts so easily. She was glad her reflexes were sharp despite everything, although this was a reminder she couldn't afford to let her emotions affect her performance on the job.

"Belmont is a threat to this town," Lincoln bellowed. A vein bulged in his neck and his face was redder than Rudolf's nose. The man was going to have a heart attack if he didn't get a grip on his temper. "You have to put a stop to it."

"We might as well talk out here." Chief Slayton sighed as he came forward to meet the mayor. "It'll save me having to repeat it all later."

And he's probably afraid he'll strangle the mayor if he has him alone in his office, Joey thought.

"Belmont stalked my wife." His voice vibrated with rage and he kept flexing his fists. "He harassed her all the way from the hair salon until she ducked into Buckley's Service Station. She was beside herself when she got home and told me about it."

The hair appointment explained why Mrs. Lincoln had skipped the coffee club meeting that morning.

The mayor continued his tirade. "That man's a menace, I tell you." Lincoln stopped to catch his breath, looked at all four police officers for agreement, but didn't wait for it. "Under the circumstances, I couldn't very well continue to have Verna Belmont working under my roof. I had to terminate her on the spot. That poor woman lost her job and it's her husband's fault."

Great. Joey wanted to drop her head in her hands but locked her body at attention. Lincoln had to use the wife to get back at her idiot husband. As if it was Verna's fault. As if she had any control. Just like Sammy told them. The mayor didn't think about how his decisions might impact others. He didn't give any thought to what an unhappy Christmas this would be for the Belmont kids.

She didn't need to see the chief's signal to go pick up the troubled man. Good Lord, where would this tragedy end?

Chapter Nine

They were on their way to the Belmont house again, which put a knot in Fletch's gut. Looking into the faces of those little kids was too hard. The last time he'd been bringing their father back. How bad was it going to be this time, taking him away? He glanced at his partner.

She hadn't even put up a fight for the keys and was staring out the window, giving him the silent treatment. At least that made it easier to think about how he could make things up to her. If Joey could shoot fire from her eyes, he'd have been ashes on the floor after the meeting with Rufus. And he knew if she ever decided to shoot him for real, he was a dead man. Her reflexes were amazing when Lincoln had burst into the station like a raving idiot. Even with her body angled away from the door, Jo was positioned and ready to fire ahead of him and Wedge.

He had no doubts left, after their night together, that Joey Frost was the only woman for him. He'd come to work humming like a teenager.

How had he managed to get from heaven to hell in less than six hours? Then, when she avoided coming to the station in the morning, he'd started to worry that she regretted being with him. Worry turned to uncertainty. Was she having doubts? Was it just a fling for her? A knot formed in his gut. It would be easier to face an enemy combatant than rejection from the woman he loved.

Then, the mayor had called with more of his crap. Fletch was sure it was the boy again and had jumped the gun. Joey wouldn't believe him, but he'd done what he thought was right for the boy when he'd talked to Rufus. He would have included her if she'd been around, but he acted within his rights as her superior officer. She was mad now, but once she understood, she'd get over it. He hoped.

A few minutes later, he and Joey stood on the doorstep of the Belmont house for the second time in a week. He desperately hoped the children weren't around to see the police drag their father off to jail the day before Christmas.

Oliver Belmont was not sober when he answered the door, but had not completely disappeared into the bottle yet, either. He stared at them with rheumy eyes, almost as if he were expecting them.

Fletch took the lead. "Mr. Belmont, we need you to come with us to answer some questions regarding an incident this morning. Is there someone else in the house to look after the children?" It didn't look like Verna had come directly home when she left the Lincolns' home, which made their job easier, but it also posed a problem. Fletch hoped the older man had child care alternatives.

Fortunately, Belmont was sober enough to

remember. "Neighbor'll take 'em 'til the wife gets back."

"That's Mrs. White, isn't it?" Joey asked.

When Belmont nodded, Joey appealed to Fletch with her eyes. She flicked her gaze down the hall behind Belmont, where the seven- and nine year old kids stood watching and listening, their solemn little faces pale but dry eyed.

His heart shrank a size in his chest. Crap, she was leaving him to deal with the kids. Was this revenge? No, she cared too much about her people to do anything other than what she thought was best for them. What was she trying to do?

"Why don't I run over and see if she's home while Mr. Belmont gets his coat and lets his kids know when their mother will be home?" Joey said, pointedly and caught Fletch's eye.

He gave her a slow nod. Message received and acknowledged. These kids needed some reassurance from their father that they weren't being abandoned, that their mother was coming home soon. They needed to hear it from their parent. They needed to believe that their world was still safe and secure—even if it wasn't the truth. He saw some of the tension bleed out of her before she turned away from him and headed next door.

The kids gathered in the living room as their father explained he was leaving. To Fletch's surprise, Belmont's tone was gentle and he hugged each one, reassuring them there was no need to worry. To give them some semblance of privacy, Fletch assessed the room. The Christmas tree was dressed with the paper snowflakes he'd seen the kids working on during his last visit, and there was wrapping paper, tape and scissors on the floor. But there didn't seem to be any presents under the tree.

He felt a small finger poke into his thigh. It was one of Belmont's youngest boys, his eyes pooling with unshed tears. "Will you make sure Santa knows where to find Daddy this Christmas?"

Fletch had never taken a punch to the stomach as powerful as that child's words. He had no answer. The elderly Mrs. White saved him when she bustled into the living room. She had Christmas shortbread in a tin and sent the kids down the hall to the kitchen to wash their hands and wait for her at the table. She reassured Joey that the children would be fine in her care until Verna Belmont got home—they were well behaved, and the older ones tended to the younger ones quite well, she told them. Joey left her cell phone number in case any problems arose.

Once the kids were out of the room, Belmont wasn't as cooperative, but Joey convinced him it wouldn't take long to get the paperwork out of the way so he could return home. Fletch thought they were lucky to arrive before the man was fully in the bag or the situation may have turned nasty. Finally, with Belmont in the back seat, Fletch took the wheel. Joey turned away from him again to gaze out the window. The sun was bouncing off the snow and the street was decorated for the holidays, but Fletch had left his heart in the sad little bungalow at the end of Spruce Street.

As they slowed to turn left at the traffic light near Main Street, Joey nudged him and twisted around to look at the building they were just passing.

"What is it?" he asked.

She kept her voice low. "The kids came out the

side door of the community hall. We've gotta make this quick. I don't want them seeing her father being led into jail without an explanation."

She meant Sammy and Ivy. They just couldn't get a break. He would have dropped his head on the steering wheel if he wasn't driving. Instead, he hit the gas and pulled around to the back of the station. Joey was out before he'd put it into *Park*.

"I've gotta tell her before she hears it from someone else, okay?"

"Yeah, sure. I can take care of this." It was the least he could do. He watched her disappear up the side of the station and wondered how often he would have to watch her walk away from him before it would stop hurting.

~~~

It was such a clear day, Joey could see the teens two blocks down the street. They were facing each other on the sidewalk in front of the White Pine Community Hall. Ivy suddenly wiped her cheeks with mittened hands and gave her boyfriend a hug, before she spun away and ran down the street toward home.

Sammy turned to stare at the town hall across the square. Joey feared the Lincoln statue might lose its head altogether this time.

"Sammy!" she yelled to get his attention before his anger morphed into destructive action again. "Sammy?"

Sometimes rage can close down all the other senses, so she couldn't say whether Sammy didn't hear her shout or if he ignored it. But he bolted and disappeared behind the school. Nothing propels a body through heavy, wet snow like unbridled fury. She gave up any thought of catching up with him and reversed directions to return to the station at a less hurried pace.

Poor kids. Joey rubbed her chest where her own heart ached. She remembered the pain of first love. She didn't realize it only got worse as an adult. At sixteen, when she thought she couldn't live without Fletch, she'd had her family for support. She remembered Garret trying, however awkwardly, to be sympathetic. Her eldest brother had found her crying from a broken heart in one of the barns. He'd given her a hug and told her to find a boy her own age, who'd stick around for the long haul. Thinking about his words now, he had given her the same message he'd already given Fletch. Still she couldn't find it in her heart to be angry with him.

Garret's later loss of his wife and unborn child had been so much greater. She so hoped his new relationship with Lily Parker might give him and his sweet little son the Christmas gift they yearned for most. If only a wish could bring Sammy Lincoln and Ivy Belmont a happy holiday. Their adult fathers were so caught up in their feud, they were acting like children. Their families were in turmoil. At least Sammy and Ivy had each other.

Fletch wasn't at his desk when she returned so she assumed he'd gone to the courthouse to file the paperwork on Oliver Belmont. The thought of the father spending the holidays in jail while his young family tried to celebrate the day without him left her feeling cranky. Drunk or not, his kids loved and needed their dad.

The holiday carols playing on repeat were starting to annoy her. Carols were fine in stores, and churches, and places where you brought joy to the world and peace on earth, but that didn't seem to be part of her job lately. She pulled up the Baby Doe file to update and, seeing the contact for family services, pulled out her cell to do another check-in before they closed their office for the holidays.

~ ~ ~

It was snowing heavily again an hour later when Fletch returned to the station. He pushed open the door of the station and stamped the snow off his feet on the mat. Carol Falls was definitely having a white Christmas this year.

"Close the door!" Wedge shouted. "You tryin' to heat the whole town?"

"Too much of a sissie to handle a little draft, Wedge?" Fletch let go of the door as he pushed his hood off. He could joke now that he felt he'd accomplished something positive over at the courthouse.

Taylor called, "Don't let the dog out," just as the beast darted past him before the door fully closed.

Fletch groaned at the thought of having to go back out to find the mutt. He had his hand on the door when the familiar, dreaded sound of skidding tires on wet pavement penetrated the white noise of the patrol room.

For an instant, everyone froze, waiting for the inevitable impact.

Fletch yanked open the door, reflexes and instinct kicking into high alert.

Joey was out of her chair as the sound of metal thudded into flesh.

Wedge was on their heels as they shot out the door, just as the dog's piteous howl rose and suddenly stopped.

Joey's voice at his shoulder cut through it all, "Nooo—"

Hitting the sidewalk, they all skidded to a halt and scanned through the snowfall until they spotted the '78 Buick—the car Fletch remembered Mr. Ingram driving earlier in the week—the day Joey let the old man off with a warning instead of insisting he get a medical for his license.

The dog was nowhere in sight. Fletch clamped his jaw shut. How had he let the damn dog slip by him? He'd been distracted, pining about Joey being so close but out of his reach. And pretending to be one of the guys by joking with Wedge.

Joey shot past him and slid to a halt against the driver's side door of the vehicle. He realized she hadn't stopped to grab her jacket or gloves. She pulled open the car door and began checking the old man for injuries. She was focused on the job, but he knew she hadn't forgotten her dog. She'd never forgive him for letting Buddy get out. As he rounded the front of the car, he spotted the smudge of red on the left headlight. If Buddy was beyond help, Joey didn't need to see it. Fletch signaled Wedge to check.

He shrugged off his parka and tucked it around Joey's shoulders. She didn't seem to be aware her whole body was trembling. She was squatting beside Mr. Ingram speaking into her mobile phone. "Okay, we'll see you in twenty."

He waited until she had flicked her thumb to end the call, before asking, "How is he?"

Joey laid a gentle hand on the old man's cheek and, with a reassuring smile, replied. "He got quite a fright but he's going to be fine. We're just going to send him to Stowe Hospital to be checked out."

The victim smiled weakly as if her word was the law and couldn't possibly be wrong.

When Ingram's eyes drifted shut, she stood upright. She gave Fletch a slight shrug and looked worried when she whispered, "He's lost some movement on one side. Could be the cold, or he might have had a stroke."

At that moment, Wedge walked up to them and handed her an emergency blanket, which she carefully placed around her charge before continuing. "His pulse is strong though...and he's lucid." With her face mask-white, she looked at her fellow officer then and asked in a tight voice, "What about Buddy?"

Wedge put an arm around her shoulder. She leaned into him. A shot of jealousy kicked Fletch in the gut but he shut it down. She needed comfort now and he didn't seem to be the one she wanted it from.

"Buddy's still breathing but I don't know how bad the injuries are. She was thrown quite a ways," Wedge said, rubbing her arm to reassure her.

They all looked in the direction of his chin point to a blanket-covered mound a few feet away. The black tail poking out was motionless.

Joey's raspy inhale gave away her grief. She took a step toward the injured dog, then stopped herself and looked at the elderly man in the car. She squeezed her eyes shut for an instant and took a deep breath. She said nothing but remained beside the car.

Helpless wasn't something Fletch was used to feeling, and he didn't like it now. With a little tug, he eased Joey away from Ingram so Wedge could take over.

He held her chin in his hand to get her attention. "I wish I could tell you everything will be okay, but I can't do that." He'd never had a pet but he understood that for many people they were like a member of the family. A guy in his unit wired flowers to his mother in Ohio when the family cat died. "I know both Mr. Ingram and Buddy mean a lot to you, so you tell me who you need to be with right now. We're all here to help." It broke his heart to see her look from one to the other, her eyes shimmering. But she squared her shoulders and nodded to the car. He held her cold cheeks in both hands, and smiled at her. "I'll take care of Buddy for you, sweetheart. You take care of Ingram. Wedge can look after the scene. I'll call you as soon as I know how Buddy's doing."

Gratitude swept across her face as her lips trembled.

~~~

Joey spent several hours pacing in the hospital waiting room with nothing to do but worry about Mr. Ingram and think about what an idiot she was. She'd already notified the Ladies Auxiliary to look after Mrs. Ingram's care. The doctor who saw Mr. Ingram in Emergency, agreed with her suspicion of a small stroke. At least Fletch hadn't started with I Told You So.

She wanted to be mad, but couldn't work up the energy. Besides he was right. For all she knew, the lack of circulation to the brain was the cause of his accelerated mental deterioration. If she'd insisted on the medical before letting him keep his license, none of this would have happened. She'd nearly killed him with kindness. And might have killed Buddy, too. *If Buddy dies, it's my fault.*

By the time she got back to town, the snow had

stopped falling and Wedge had cleared Ingram's car off the road. There was nothing more she could do at the station, so she headed back out the door. When her cell phone rang, she picked up her pace as she grabbed it without bothering checking the display. "I'm on my way to you now, Fletch."

"No point, Jo—"

Joey caught her breath and stopped moving, afraid to hear the rest.

"—The vet is taking Buddy into surgery now. X-rays show a bad break to her front leg."

He paused, and Joey waited, unable to ask the hard question."

"Buddy's hanging in, but the vet isn't sure yet if there is internal bleeding or other damage we can't see." Joey could hear the gentleness in Fletch's tone over the phone. "I don't think it will help if you sit here and worry, Jo."

"I should be there—"

The hitch in her voice stopped her from saying more.

"There's nothing for you to do right now and you're only going to wear yourself out pacing in the waiting room. I'm running over to see Aunt Elle for an hour or so. Then I'll come back here and check in. I promise I'll call you as soon as there's anything to know."

Joey stood on the icy sidewalk outside the station, vibrating with nervous energy, not sure what to do. She went inside to do paperwork, thinking it would keep her mind busy. That only worked for a short time. The cell phone lay silent on her desk. She picked it up ready to hit speed dial, but stopped herself. If he said he'd call, he would call. There was nothing to be gained by nagging him or the vet. She desperately needed to find a release for the pressure building inside her, before she exploded like an overheating steam engine. She got up and grabbed her jacket.

As soon as she hit the sidewalk, the frosty air hit her lungs and the bright sun warmed her face. Out of long habit, she walked east fixing her gaze on the snow-capped mountains in the distance. She cut across Cedar Road. As the shock of the last few hours enveloped her, she reached her destination, the Village Green.

By nature, Joey considered herself an optimistic person. However, some days life just sucked. Today was one of them. She wished she could just keep going past the covered bridge, out of town. She could re-start her life somewhere else. Had she made a mistake when she chose to settle in her small home town? The urge to travel had never beckoned her the way it had Kate Wedge. Kate became a globetrotting journalist. So she had adventures in foreign lands to measure against life in Carol Falls when she made her decision to return. Fletch also had the choice after he finished his tour of duty. He chose Boston.

She shoved her hands into her jacket pockets and watched each foot as she placed one in front of the other. She ached with the urge to wrap her arms around Buddy's neck. To ease the pain, she thought about adopting the dog if the owner didn't show up after Christmas. The bungalow was a bit lonely, and Buddy had been a better partner than Fletch the last few days. Carol Falls had never had a K-9 unit, and Buddy was really smart. Admittedly, Fletch had been kind about Buddy, and Joey really appreciated it, but they still didn't trust each other. Without that, they couldn't be partners, friends, or lovers. It was probably for the best that he was leaving.

At least, the fling with Fletch had been private, and short lived, so her brothers wouldn't be teasing her about it. She wondered if she could spend the holidays at the police station. Both her brothers were paired up this year, one newly married and the other in a promising relationship. Christmas dinner with the family was going to be a painful night for her. The only single adult at the table. How pathetic was that?

When she reached the bridge, she peered through its shadows to the world beyond, to life outside her home town, then turned to follow the uneven path through the park and headed back to the station, and the community she served and loved.

As she passed the town's Christmas tree, her mind went full circle, bouncing to the subject of adoptions again. This time, it was baby Holly who had her attention. The Vandal Gogh case was closed but the clock was still ticking on Baby Doe, although over the few days she'd had the file, the effort had become less about competing with Fletch to close the case and all about a tiny little girl who needed her missing mother found. She glanced up at the pretty tree lights but didn't feel her usual swell of delight. Her thoughts stayed mired in gloom. She stretched her arms behind her, hoping more room for oxygen in her chest might snuff out the darkness in her heart. Maybe if she sorted out baby Holly's life by Christmas, she'd feel more optimistic about her ability to untangle her own. But there was still nothing from the lab on any of the evidence. The talk of 'swaddling' was exciting but she didn't have any idea how it got her closer to finding the birth mother.

As she rounded the tree, Joey's internal radar picked up a presence on the bench nearby. Whoever it was, she really wasn't in the mood to chat. For this once, she hoped she could just give them a nod and keep going. She wanted to be alone.

When the shadow didn't move, concern made her step off the path, squinting into the gloom. It was the same bench where Fletch had waited for her once before. Long ago.

The present smashed into the past. This time, he sat with an unnatural stillness in the fading light. She imagined he had learned to stand guard for long hours without giving away his presence to enemy eyes. She stopped and stood facing him, hugging herself. The muscles in her throat cramped, making it hard for her to choke out even one word.

"Buddy?"

"—is out of surgery. The vet wants to keep an eye on her at least for the night."

Joey's heart crashed into her ribs. "But she's out of danger?"

"Still in recovery, so we have to wait a while longer to be sure everything is okay. But the vet seemed confident she'd be fine once the cast and stitches are removed. "

"I'm going to keep her, Fletch. If no one comes to claim her." Why she was telling him, she didn't know. Maybe to acknowledge the commitment to herself. There was still a small chance the original owner might show up to claim the dog, but the seven-day impoundment period was ticking by quickly.

He smiled. "I know."

They stared at each other for another moment

longer, until he broke the silence.

"I processed Belmont and got him released on his own recognizance. He can still be with his family over Christmas."

A small ray of light broke through the gloom she'd been carrying. "That's really good. His family deserves to be together for Christmas."

It was also impossibly fast. He must have run it from one office to the next at the court house and found every person he needed at their desk. And now, if anything happened within a mile of the mayor over the holidays, Fletch's job would be on the line. Why did he do it?

He got up from the bench and moved toward her. He was watching her too closely, his face unreadable. "You were right about this last incident, Joey. Belmont readily admits to all the trouble he's been giving the mayor, and he even acknowledges he went too far when he scared Mrs. Lincoln. He realized it when she ran into the service station, but it was too late to apologize."

Fletch stopped a couple of feet from her, but his eyes stayed steady on hers. The fist around her heart tightened its grip. He looked like he was hurting too. That couldn't be right.

"We didn't get a chance to talk before the mayor interrupted us earlier."

Another thought had occurred to her during her walk. When it came to acting like a good partner, she wasn't a shiny pot either—but she was not as black as Fletch's kettle. She held out for another second or two of silence before she gave in and took a step closer. "If this is about not reporting in this morning, I admit I was wrong to go off without telling you. I should have phoned to say I was staying to look for Sammy and to interview the ladies' coffee club. It was a spur of the moment thing. I saw them there and suddenly thought they would know stuff they weren't saying about the abandoned baby. I wasn't trying to cut you out. But it just wasn't somewhere you could go with me anyway. And they wouldn't have talked with you there."

She stopped and looked at the ground, giving the snow a kick with the toe of her boot. "That's no excuse for not keeping my partner apprised of my whereabouts in case you needed me."

An apology didn't count unless you looked the injured person in the eye—at least that was the rule in the Frost household. So she took a deep breath, and raised her chin. It took sheer force of will to make her eyes meet his as she said, "I'm sorry, and I won't let it happen again."

"No problem." He nodded but didn't move away. His hands were shoved in his pockets and he was hunched into his jacket.

"Is there something else on your mind?"

Fletch squared his shoulders.

She was puzzled. Was he finally going to admit to her what she already knew? He was leaving in a few months.

"You didn't give me a chance to update you on your cases. When I got the call this morning about the dog sh—crap, on the mayor's doorstep, I assumed it was Sammy. It met your criteria— directed at Lincoln personally, not as the mayor. I didn't think about his wife opening the door. I don't know this town like you do, so I talked to Rufus about both situations to get his advice on how to proceed. We both felt it would be best to let the mayor know his son was acting out so he could arrange for appropriate counseling."

Joey chewed her lip. If she'd been around, she knew he would have run it by her instead to see if she agreed. He didn't need to say it.

"A little pile of dog crap really isn't so important you can't wait for the lead investigator—who is also your partner. There's no excuse for you and the chief discussing it and taking action without me. The whole point is that the lead investigator has insight and knowledge of the case that could avoid unforeseen repercussions."

He didn't flinch or try to argue.

She fisted her hands in her pockets, but managed not to raise her voice. "What I think is that you and Rufus talked it over and figured the sooner Lincoln knew about Sammy, the better the mayor could manage any fallout that might damage his reputation. No need to include me on that, of course, since it has *nothing* to do with the case."

"A parent knows what's best for their child, Jo. The police have to notify the parent when a minor is involved. You know this is what had to be done. It was just a question of when."

The case was closed and none of this really mattered anymore. From the way he was rubbing his forehead like she had given him a headache, he knew it too. They stood face to face, but apart.

She watched him while trying to keep her face from giving away her emotions. Knowing what was coming. Not wanting to talk about it. Hoping she wouldn't react. Because it wasn't anger she was feeling, but hurt. Anger she could express...but hurt might leak out as tears.

If he wasn't going to tell her the truth—he was

leaving—she might as well throw it out on the table. "What I know, Fletch, is that I can't trust you. You say one thing and then do something else. Or you simply don't say anything at all and let someone else get hurt. But it doesn't matter because you're leaving in a couple of months anyway. You just forgot to tell me—again."

She didn't feel she owed him the rest of *her* truth. That all it had taken was one night in his arms and she'd fallen in love with him more deeply than she was capable of at sixteen—only to find out he was leaving in a couple of months. It was happening all over again. She loved him and he was leaving her. And it hurt too much. Joey turned, ready to leave him, but he grabbed her elbow so fast she didn't get to move a step.

"Please, Jo, don't walk away. I can explain why I talked to the chief. And I'll explain about the job. But we can't work anything out if we keep walking away from each other." He gestured toward the bench. "Let's see if we can, at least, understand each other."

His hold on her was loose so she could pull away. He would let her go if she wanted to. But behind his strength, she sensed his sadness and hurt might be as deep as her own. Maybe they could close the door on their relationship without the pain this time. Maybe if they understood each other, losing him wouldn't hurt as much.

She nodded and let him lead her to the bench.

"I'm sorry I didn't talk to you before I went to the chief. I know we can't agree on what I did but I do want you to believe I only did it because I was afraid for the boy."

"Afraid for Sammy?"

"Jo, all I can tell you is that when I got the call this morning, it *felt* urgent to me. I've thought about it since, trying to figure out why it suddenly seemed like life and death. I guess I still carry some baggage from my tours overseas." He looked past her, seeing things that took place at another time, and thousands of miles away. "There were so many kids trapped by the politics and greed over there. All things they couldn't understand or didn't have any control over. There was nothing I could do to help them. I just can't believe that, in our own country, without a war to blame, we can't take care of our children. Get child care, food and clothes for those Belmont kids, or help Sammy deal with his anger in a safe, healthy way."

He angled toward her. "Jo, I swear to you, I'm trying to do the same thing you are. I just can't do it the same way. I'm a guy who lives within the rules. It's all I know."

His voice with thick with emotion and he reached out to her but stopped himself. Instead, he shoved his hands into his pockets again and slid into an uncharacteristic slouch on the bench.

Joey wanted desperately to wrap her arms around him. While it might give them both temporary comfort, distrust would still loom between them as an insurmountable barrier. Without trust she couldn't tell him what was in her heart, so she crossed her arms and leaned back on the bench as well. The stars had come out, and one shone more brightly than the rest. It seemed to be right above Carol Falls, shining like the Star of Bethlehem, ready to lead some lost soul to the safety of their small town. If only a star could help them find their way, Joey thought. Without it, they'd have to find their own way.

Without sitting up or looking at him, she tried to explain what she hardly understood herself. "I'm ticked about you jumping the gun, Fletch, but that isn't what is happening here. I don't have to trust you at work, or even as a...friend...because you plan to walk out of my life again. Will it be another ten years before you show up in town again without warning? I can't be...with...someone who keeps secrets and makes decisions without including me, Fletch."

The corner of her heart, where she'd been jamming all her inconvenient emotions, was getting too full to contain them so she stood up to leave while she still had her dignity. "We're too different to be anything to each other. So you don't owe me any explanation about the job."

Before he could give her a response, Fletch's cell phone buzzed. He swore under his breath, as he reached for it.

Joey's went off too. Her call was from Wedge. "Joey. Get back to the station. The mayor's kid is missing."

Chapter Ten

After they raced into the patrol room, Joey first asked if she could get Mayor Lincoln anything to eat or drink. He shook his head, incoherent sounds gurgling up from his throat. There was no evidence of the suave politician in the distraught father pacing the patrol room. His blonde hair stood on end from raking his fingers through it, his face was marble white, and his eyes were glassy with shock. He swiped his lips with his tongue and gripped her arms with both hands. Desperation wafted off him as he pleaded, "Help me. You know him better than I do. You can find him for me."

Chief Slayton handed her a torn off sheet of lined, yellow paper. She felt Fletch at her elbow as she read it.

I can't take this anymore.

If you won't accept me for who I am,

then there's no point trying anymore.

I'm sorry I'll never see you again.

Fletch steadied her hand with his as she read it

over a second time, hoping there was a clue to the boy's whereabouts hidden somewhere in his words. Their personal differences slipped away without conscious thought, replaced by the demands for their training and skills.

"What does it mean?" The mayor slumped in a chair someone had pulled up for him, and Taylor handed him a glass of water. Wedge stood by, looking from his boss to Joey and then Fletch, ready to move as soon as he was given orders.

"Trouble," she and Fletch said under their breath, but then Fletch signaled Joey to take the lead. Easier for the parent to focus on questions from one person.

"Mr. Lincoln," Joey snapped, hoping a sharp voice would break through his shock. "When and where did you find this note?"

He straightened in his chair and looked at her, clearly working to give them what they needed. He looked at his watch and replied in a careful, hoarse whisper. "Fifteen minutes ago. It was on his bed."

"When did you last see Sammy?"

"About ten o'clock this morning—" He looked at Chief Slayton. "—not long after your call." His chin sank onto his chest. A sob racked him. The chief gripped the politician's shoulder tightly which seemed to give him the strength to continue. "We had words and it got ugly. He was mad I'd fired Verna Belmont. I didn't see why it was his business." He gulped in another sob. "He told me Belmont's daughter was his girlfriend. I just couldn't believe it, and told him not to see her anymore."

"Did he give you any indication—" Joey looked for a softer word, but had to push on. "—he might want to harm himself?"

The bleak pain in the father's eyes told her he'd been asking himself that same question. "I just don't know." He shook his head from side to side like a caged animal. "I guess I haven't been paying much attention. I just don't know anything about my son anymore. We didn't notice he was missing until my wife went to see if he was hungry."

The four officers looked down at the bowed head of their mayor, then at each other and finally, at Joey. They were hoping her knowledge of the boy would give them something to go on, some way to find him. Joey blamed herself. She should have acted on her suspicions sooner. She should have done something to prevent this. But there was no time for that now. It was clear they all feared the worst and valuable time had been lost.

"Wedge, take Mr. Lincoln home and start calling kids from the school. See if anyone has seen Sammy today." Wedge gave her a tight nod, and then surprised Joey with his gentleness as he eased the sobbing father out of his chair.

"Fletch, you're with me. Chief, you'll coordinate from here as the command post, right?" When he nodded, she added, already heading for the door, "We'll keep you in the loop."

Fletch took the wheel so she could work out her search strategy. He flicked on the flashing lights to save time getting through holiday traffic. "Where are we going?"

"The Belmonts'. Ivy is the key to this." She was thinking out loud, more than explaining. When he eased around the traffic circle she looked over at the speedometer, ready to tell him to punch it. When she saw the needle, she kept silent. *This man can drive. Maybe he'd teach me later. Before he leaves.* She pushed that thought away before it distracted her.

"Any chance he's there with her?" Fletch asked. His voice was quiet and even.

She shook her head. "Doubt it. He wouldn't have left a note like that if he was. But she's our best bet for finding him quickly."

They pulled up in front of the Belmont house in record time. She'd kept her mouth shut when he'd driven the wrong way down a one-way street and cut the corner off Willow Road by going through the gas station parking lot. Apparently Fletch could break a few rules when it suited him.

She jumped out of the vehicle with Fletch on her heels, but took a deep breath before rapping on the front door. Verna Belmont opened it. Her eyes were puffy and red, her face slack with exhaustion. Her shoulders drooped as if the weight she carried had finally become too much for her slight body to bear.

"We're sorry to intrude, Verna," Joey said. "May we come in?"

The older woman wiped her palms down the front of her beige house dress before ushering them inside. She led them into the living room.

Joey glanced at the Belmonts' Christmas tree. It was covered in an odd assortment of ornaments made from kids' craft supplies, and underneath were packages marked FROM SANTA, wrapped with bright foil paper, sealed with tape bearing a discreet Frost Farm logo. On every one was a big red tag stencilled with a child's name. Joey closed her eyes and sent a silent blessing to Verna and Ivy's caring creativity, and her own parents for their

Christmas Basket program. Without it, there wouldn't be anything under the tree for the Belmont children this year. At the top of the tree, she noticed the worn-out star was blinking erratically, looking like it would go out any moment, like Sammy's young life might if they didn't find him quickly. Joey blinked back tears. She had to focus on the more immediate crisis.

Verna's husband immediately got to his feet as they entered. "Officers?" He fidgeted and seemed to shrink. Poor man. He thought they were there for him again. His wife stood by wringing her hands, probably assuming the same thing. What a way to spend Christmas Eve.

The toddler's quilt Joey had seen on the last visit was neatly folded on the arm of the couch. It seemed so familiar Joey picked it up and fingered the fabric. On closer inspection, it was actually made from dozens of pieces of fabric, some with tiny pink, yellow and blue flowers, another with gingham stripes, others were baby blue plaid, all stitched together by hand.

"This is beautiful." Joey said, hoping to put the parents at ease.

Oliver spoke up with pride in his voice. "Verna has a fine hand with a needle. She's made one of those for each of our kids."

Something had clearly caused a change in the man if he was talking about his wife's handiwork.

"Please, sit down." Oliver's voice was quiet but clear. He seemed sober, and it was late afternoon. A good sign. Verna added, "Can I get you some tea?"

"Oh, no thanks," Joey said. "We're actually hoping to speak to Ivy if she's here."

"Ivy?" Both parents looked at her, their

concern evident in their sudden stiffness. Despite their present difficulties, these two parents were ready to protect their children.

"One of her school friends is missing and we're hoping she can help us find him."

Ivy didn't answer when Verna called up the stairs, and with a sinking stomach Joey followed Verna up to the room the girl shared with her younger sister.

The room had one window, faded wallpaper, and was barely large enough to hold the two single beds. The bedding was threadbare but, at the foot of each, lay a small patchwork quilt like the one downstairs. With a sigh, Joey recognized them as a physical token of a mother's love and devotion to each child despite their hardships.

Joey knew what to look for, so she immediately saw the pink envelop on Ivy's pillow. The teen had made sure her sister wouldn't read the note by sealing it, and printing neatly on the front, *For Mom & Dad ONLY*.

Inside was much the same as what Sammy had written:

I have to go with Sammy.

I can't live without him.

And Daddy's right,

the family will be better off

with one less mouth to feed.

Verna Belmont gasped and would have fallen if Fletch hadn't come up behind them. He caught her and eased her over to the other twin bed. Her husband pushed his way into the tiny room. "What is it? What is it?"

All parents, rich or poor, suddenly were the

same when their child is at risk, Joey thought as she looked at the couple. She shielded Oliver from seeing his daughter's words, probably unintentionally hurtful, by handing the note to Fletch. She gave them the news that Ivy had a boyfriend who was also missing, and their intentions were unknown. In their distress, they didn't ask the name of the boyfriend so Joey didn't volunteer it. It would be tragic if the desperate act of children was what brought an end to the friction between the Lincolns and the Belmonts. Or would it cement the rift if the kids weren't found in time?

Joey repeated the same questions she'd asked Sammy's father. Verna was more attuned to Ivy than Sammy's parent had been to his son, but she'd been working long hours out of the home since the fall. She had noticed her daughter was moodier than usual over the last month, yet Verna was shocked to find out Ivy had been skipping classes to care for her siblings. She didn't know, or Joey suspected didn't want to know, that her husband's drinking had reached a point that made him unreliable as a caregiver, at least in the eyes of their eldest daughter. As with the Lincolns, Joey instructed them to stay at home in case their daughter called.

She and Fletch pulled up in front of the police station and had to push through the gathering volunteers on the sidewalk. The police chief must have pulled in the rest of the officers, and sent out word that volunteers were needed to search for missing children. Everyone in Carol Falls dropped whatever they were doing to answer that call. A burst of pride, in her town and in her neighbors surged above the wave of fear pulsing through her.

Joey notified her boss of the second missing

teen, and sat with the rest of the team leaders to set out the search grid. Harold and Garrett were already out searching the Frost property, especially the Sugar Shack and other out-buildings, and would make sure the kids weren't anywhere along Maple Farm Road. With other teams fanning out to the south, Fletch and Joey would go east toward the school and community center, and would cover the middle of town, from Carol River, south and west to the Village Green. With the plans set, the search began.

~~~

The temperature had dropped considerably, once the sun set, and the wind was picking up. They listened to another radio report of a completed search grid without success. Joey's teeth began to chatter from the cold, or possibly fear.

Fletch turned up the car heater, and reached for Joey's hand. A slight tremor in his hand made her look at him. The expression on his face scared her. Despite the cold, his skin was pale and he looked like he was running a fever. His lips were barely visible he had clamped them so tightly.

"Fletch? Are you okay?"

"I didn't think I'd have to deal with this here. Not in Carol Falls."

She waited for him to say more, but he seemed to have gone inside his head. She couldn't imagine Fletch being afraid of any kind of case. Certainly not runaway kids. It was the dread etched on his face that told her what he was thinking. "They aren't dead, Fletch. We're going to find them. I know we are."

She wished there was some way she could convince him she was right. "It's Christmas Eve,

Fletch. Nothing bad can happen on Christmas Eve. It's against the laws of nature."

His smile was bitter. "That's one law I wish was written in stone, sweetheart. But I can tell you first-hand it isn't." He looked off into the distance again. It was a few minutes before Fletch took a deep breath. He gripped her hand as if she might jump out of the jeep and run away if he let go.

Their nerves were raw by the time they reached the last grid in their search zone, Lincoln Village Green. They sat in the car staring out the windshield at the giant Christmas tree twinkling with bright colored lights.

"The Village Green is four blocks of open space." Joey said. "There's an electrical shed, but it's secured with a deadbolt and padlock. Nothing else except the outdoor rink."

"And the river on the far side," said Fletch.

They looked at each other, both afraid to accept the unspoken possibility.

"Are you sure there isn't somewhere else they might go? Where did you go at their age when you ran away from home?" Fletch paused, and she could feel him scanning her face, before he added, "When I hurt you, where did you go to be alone?"

She wished she could just forget everything about the weeks after he left her. She still wanted them to make a clean break this time. "Don't look so guilty, Fletch. I was a hormonal teenage girl. I felt *everything* like it was the end of the world." She'd meant to be flippant but there was an edge to her voice. She tried again. "I thought I was in love with you and then you threw me away. It hurt. I lived. End of story."

Suddenly, a forgotten memory resurfaced, just

as he'd intended with his question. Joey pointed to the red covered bridge across from the park. "There. That's where I went after you left. After Garret caught me crying in the barn, I had to find somewhere more private. I'd hide under the bridge and listen to the sound of cars driving over. It was actually quite hypnotic."

The initial rush of adrenalin subsided just as suddenly. "But, Fletch, it was early summer. The kids would die of the cold there before they'd have a chance to do themselves any harm."

"Maybe that's the idea." He spoke quietly, more to himself than her. "To sleep under Heaven's watch."

Joey looked at him. It wasn't something she'd ever heard from him before. The military *had* changed him.

When he realized he'd spoken out loud, he explained, "My father said that once when I was a boy. I overheard him telling my mom that some of his buddies' bodies couldn't be recovered and returned home. She cried but my father told her, it didn't matter where they lay, because they were sleeping under Heaven's watch."

Joey didn't know what to say as her throat tightened.

Fletch grabbed the emergency blankets and met Joey at the front of the vehicle, then they headed off together into the dark silent park. The fresh fall of snow was up to Joey's knees in places. As the ground began to slope down toward the river, she sank up to her hips. The beam of Fletch's flashlight caught her in the eyes as he grabbed her hand to pull her out. Finally, they intersected a path of fresh footprints along the side of the bridge.

"Sammy? Ivy?" Joey yelled as loud as she could. Fear vibrated through her. She couldn't imagine how she would keep her head if they were too late when they found these kids.

Fletch echoed her call, his deeper baritone voice carrying across the river before it bounced back as if mocking them. Or had someone answered their call. They both froze. He shouted again. Joey held her breath. Please be here. Please. Please.

"Here. We're over here." They found the two figures huddled under the bridge in the shadows. Ivy's face was so completely white, she was barely visible against the snow. Fletch dropped in front of her, wrapped her thin body in a blanket and held her gray-tinged cheeks in his bare hands as he murmured reassurances to her.

"Sammy, are you okay?" Joey grabbed her blanket, and wrapped the boy. "Can you move your fingers and toes?" She didn't wait for an answer. She just pulled him into her chest and hugged him.

Fletch picked Ivy up in his arms as she started to cry. Joey had to help Sammy to his feet, and heard the tremble in his voice as he assured her he could make it to the road under his own steam.

Joey got the car heater going, while Fletch tucked Ivy into the back seat, taking his parka off and wrapping it around her for added warmth.

"What were you doing under the bridge?" Joey asked to take everyone's mind off their fear.

"We were thinking we could hide out there until Boxing Day when the ski kids might give us a lift. It was the only place we thought no one would find us." Sammy glanced at Joey as if he wasn't sure yet if he was mad or glad she had. "It was getting awfully cold for Ivy, though."

He suddenly looked younger than his sixteen years. "Joey, please don't take us home."

She looked at Fletch and then at the two teenagers in the back seat.

"Sammy, your parents are frantic about you both. Whatever tensions there are between you can be worked out, I promise."

"I guess, but does it have to be tonight? We're so tired." He dropped back against his seat. His voice was weary.

Ivy reached over to take his hand, and nodded as well. "Please, Officer Frost. We just need a break for a little while."

"Fletch?" Joey didn't want to get the kids hopes up unless he was ready to agree with her.

He looked at the pale, exhausted faces and locked eyes with her. "What are you thinking?"

"Mom could take them for the night. We can sort things out with their parents in the morning."

He shrugged his agreement. "Drop me at the station so I can call off the search and let the parents know they've been found."

She smiled at him and mouthed, "That wasn't so hard, was it?"

They radioed ahead, and, in less than ten minutes, she pulled up in front of the station.

Fletch got out, turned to Joey. "Call me later."

As she watched him walk into the station, she made a call to the Frost farm to say two more children would be under her parents' roof for the night. When she flipped the cell phone closed, Ivy spoke up, "Where's Buddy, Officer Frost? I bet you would have found us faster with her help."

Joey leveled her voice so she wouldn't upset

the kids. "She had an accident today so she's still at the vet."

Sammy and Ivy leaned forward. "But she's all right, isn't she?"

Joey swallowed, and hoped she was telling the truth when she answered, "Sure, she'll be home again in no time."

After settling into their seats, Sammy spoke next. "I'm really sorry, Officer Frost. We didn't mean to cause you all this trouble."

"You're never too much trouble, Sam." Joey glanced in the rear-view mirror at the young couple huddled together in the gloom and, she suspected, holding hands underneath the blanket. "And, my shift is over, so you can just call me Joey now, like when we're at the farm." The poor boy was under enough stress, so anything that might put him more at ease was a good thing.

They drove in silence for a few minutes before she decided that talking it through might be better for them than ruminating in silence.

"Things are going to work out, you guys."

She caught Sammy's solemn nod in the mirror as he said, "I know." He didn't sound at all convinced. He gave Ivy a quick sideways look. Joey kept her eyes on the dark road to give them the illusion of privacy. The two teens whispered back and forth. Finally, Sammy poured out the story, like someone had pulled his finger from a hole in an overflowing dam. Joey let him take his time, and use his own words, without interrupting. He wrapped it up with, "Running away to get married seemed like a good idea at the time." His voice was stronger than it had been at the start.

Married? Joey had to smile. "I'm sorry to tell

you, Sam, but you two are underage so your parents would find you and get the marriage annulled."

"Are you sure?"

"Trust me, hon. There isn't anything that someone in the Frost family hasn't tried at least once. So, yeah, I'm sure." She could smile at Jimmy's escapade now, but at the time—

"I wish I had done...something," Joey said, berating herself for not speaking to Sammy as soon as she had the slightest inkling he was involved in the vandalism. She caught the teenager's attention in the rear-view again, wanting to be sure he believed her, just as another thought occurred to her. Was the family tension the only reason they'd run away to get married? She paused to think about what she should say to him, and then plunged on. "Is there anything more I need to know about what happened today so I can put things right?"

If she formally interviewed him, she'd be crossing the line—questioning minors as part of an ongoing investigation without their parents present. *Maybe my good intentions will save my job*, she thought. *No, if I ask them about a pregnancy I'm going so far over the line, only my toenails are left between me and the end of my career.* Joey felt her scarf tightening around her neck like a noose.

The light posts up ahead marked the entrance gate leading to her parents' traditional white farmhouse. She was out of time to question the kids unless she pulled over. She could hear Fletch, as if he were sitting beside her. 'Joey, you're just doing what's expedient. There's no reason you have to ask them now. Why can't you wait until their parents are present? Why can't you wait until your partner is present?' When she didn't have a good answer, she knew he was right. She pressed down on the gas pedal and drove through the gate. Who needs a conscience when you have Noel Fletcher in your head?

Frost farm was dressed up like a dollhouse. Nets of colored lights were draped over the snow-covered lilac shrubs running up both sides of the lane. The sheltering evergreen trees on either side of the house, and the entire front porch, were outlined with Christmas lights, and the final touch was a magnificent wreath on the oak door beckoning them to come on in. Just the sight of it boosted Joey's mood and put a little spring in her step. Sammy took Ivy's hand and led her up to the front door like he lived there, but stopped short of letting himself in. They stood admiring the big wreath of evergreen boughs, tied in a red velvet bow, until Joey reached over his shoulder and pushed open the front door.

Christmas music immediately assailed them as they stamped their feet on the deck of the veranda before stepping into the warmth of the inner foyer. Joey bent to unlace her boots, until she heard Ivy's quick intake of breath. She shot up straight to scrutinize the young girl's face.

"Are you going to be sick, Ivy?"

The girl did look pale under the glow of the oversized lantern chandelier hanging high over their heads, and her mouth hung open. Ivy didn't blink as she shook her head from side to side. Her voice was a whisper, as if she were in church rather than the front porch of a big old farmhouse.

"It's so beautiful."

Her words brought Joey's gaze to the scene around them, seeing it through a visitor's eyes. Just beyond the foyer a wide staircase, wrapped in garlands and ribbons, led up to the bedrooms, bathrooms, and what used to be their playroom but was now the media room. In the living room across the hall, a fire roared in the large stone hearth, with candles and thick fresh boughs draped across the mantle. The Christmas tree, a lush Fraser Fir, was fully dressed with a mishmash of decorations, many made by childish hands using construction paper, glue sticks, sparkles, markers and, in one case, a guitar string—an inspired design by her brother, Jimmy. Streams of silver tinsel danced around twinkling mini lights on every branch. To Ivy Belmont, it must seem like they'd stumbled into Santa's castle at the North Pole. Tears burned behind Joey's eyes and her ribs refused to give her lungs room to breathe. These were all things she took for granted.

Suddenly anxious to get everyone settled, Joey tapped Ivy on the shoulder and indicated she was ready to take her coat. Footsteps sounded on the second level and her mother appeared at the top of the stairs, an elegant Mrs. Claus in her crimson velvet dress and pearls.

"All set, my darlings. Sammy will be on the pull-out sofa in the spare room, and I've put Ivy in Jimmy's old room." Since it was Christmas Eve, Joey's room would already be made up for her. It had been decided—mostly by her parents, although she hadn't put up a fight—that she would still sleep at the farmhouse for the holidays. It didn't matter that she now had a home of her own in town.

Sylvia Frost hurried down the stairs, sliding one palm on the banister to steady herself. Even caught with two unexpected guest on Christmas Eve, Joey's mother managed to look sophisticated and beautiful. Her soft platinum hair was swept to one side in a twist, held in place with a sparkling clip. When she reached the foyer, she automatically wiped her hands down the front of her dress, obviously forgetting she had removed her apron earlier, before giving all three of them a hug.

"You two must be starving," Sylvia said, hustling the teenagers down the wood-paneled hall to the kitchen at the rear of the house.

Joey hung up Ivy's and Sammy's coats and followed them realizing she hadn't eaten anything since breakfast.

Sylvia's kitchen was the heart of their home. Their large farm kitchen was filled with the scent of her mother's holiday baking, some of which was hidden from her young grandson, Duncan, in the snowman cookie jar on an upper shelf. Although Sylvia had grown up as a New York City debutante, over the forty years of her marriage she'd learned from the local women how to make the most of the fresh produce. Her shelves were lined with her homemade preserves and herbs she'd dried from her garden. Black marble countertops accented the light yellow walls and oak cabinets, and, in the center of the room was a massive harvest table. It was big enough to accommodate the Frost family, as well as friends and extra farm hands who happened to be around at meal time. Joey pulled out a chair and sat down.

It wasn't long before Sammy and Ivy were polishing off sandwiches and Sylvia was setting out a plate of shortbread cookies covered in colored sprinkles and cut in the shapes of wreaths, bells and Santas. With a lush poinsettia gracing the table between them, Joey wasn't sure the kids had noticed she'd joined them.

"Thanks, Mom," she said absently, as a sandwich appeared in front of her. Then, she remembered the evidence all around her of family, love and holiday spirit. She caught her mother's hand before she moved away. The familiar green eyes radiated kindliness and intelligence, although her brow was creased in confusion, as if the words were incomprehensible.

Joey had come to realize how important they were. "I mean that, Mom. Thanks for everything."

Sylvia smiled and patted Joey's shoulder. "It's what mothers do, darling."

"Only if they can." Joey watched as her mother went past Ivy's chair and gently tucked a strand of hair behind the girl's ear. Without a word, she buttered two more slices of bread, piled on some cold cuts, cheese, and other fixings, and set the second sandwich in front of Sammy. Joey smiled as the kids' cheeks took on a healthy color, and their eyes brightened. Once she'd fueled her own body with a sandwich another idea that had been fidgeting deep in her subconscious for the last several hours finally broke through fully formed. Joey slugged down the last gulp of milk and finished her last shortbread cookie in two bites.

"Mom, could I have a quick word with you?"

~~~

Tradition was a huge part of Frost family life. Yet, tonight, when Joey told her mother what she wanted to do for Christmas dinner the next day, Sylvia had said it was time they introduced a few new traditions and had given her a hug.

The Frost household was a model of New England rural life. Harold Frost was head of the household, except when it came to the holiday festivities. It would not have occurred to him that Sylvia would do anything except carry on the Frost Family traditions, as his mother had before her. And, for almost forty years, his wife had filled the family home with holiday cheer. She made sure the lights were hung outside the farmhouse and the wreaths, on every window. She strung garlands up the staircase and over the mantle. She placed candles and candy dishes on every tabletop, made sure the silverware and crystal sparkled, the tree was dressed and appropriate presents were under it.

Yet, when Joey asked to change their traditional Frost family Christmas celebration scheduled for the very next day, her amazing mother had agreed without hesitation. Now that she'd set things in motion, it was her daughter who wasn't sure how *she* felt about letting go of the old way of celebrating the holiday. The trappings of the season she'd so taken for granted. Would her siblings be upset with her? What would her father say? When the family gathered around the dining room table every year for the Christmas feast, Harold Frost would take his place at the head, raise his glass of wine, and toast their blessings and those of past generations. Everyone would hold up their glass and solemnly repeat, 'God bless us every one'. When Joey and her brothers were small, they thought they were so grown up to be included in the toast. It was only much later that they discovered their mother had filled their glasses with grape juice—white to protect the table cloth. It was typical of her mother, though, not to leave anyone out, even the youngest.

Fletch had given her a glimpse into his life after he'd left Carol Falls. He'd understand why she needed to do this because he understood the true meaning of Christmas. He'd fought for it. She loved him for his principles, even when they made her crazy, and for his courage, his humanity, his strength—

Tears threatened. Why did he have to leave again? Before the sadness could overwhelm her, she picked up her cell phone. She had to focus on negotiating a reconciliation among people who needed her help, not on her own loneliness. Her initial phone calls paid off when both sets of parents agreed to meet at the Frost farm the next afternoon. Fletch was the harder sell, when Joey called him.

"I'm not doing this as police business or as a police officer, Fletch."

"Jo, you can't put away your badge whenever it becomes inconvenient."

"I know that, but I can't stop being a caring human being either."

"The two aren't mutually exclusive, Jo."

Joey could hear his frustration over the phone line. She was losing the argument.

"Fletch, I'm just a long time neighbor of the Lincolns and someone who cares about Ivy and Sammy." She softened her voice to take any sting out of it. "I have to do this. With or without you. But I wanted to be the one to tell you. You don't have to be here if it makes you uncomfortable or if you feel it puts you in a bad position. Remember our talk? I understand we're too different from each other. It's just who we are."

She didn't tell him how much she wanted him to be with her as moral support. She gave him the same time she'd given the parents, he promised to think about it, and they hung up. The call left her shaky, but she compensated by writing up a script for the meeting tomorrow. She really wasn't sure if the invisible line she was drawing between her personal life and her work was real or imagined in this case. If Fletch was right, or anyone involved lodged a complaint, she may not have a job in the new year. There was only so much she could plan or control. The success of her *intervention*, as she had phrased it for Fletch, would be up to the parents, and Sammy and Ivy.

Chapter Eleven

The soft melody of *What Child is This* wove its way into Joey's dream, reminding her it was Christmas Day and time to wake up. She interlaced her fingers and stretched out her arms with a huge yawn—cut off by the sharp crack of bone hitting wood. "Crap. That hurt," Joey muttered, rubbing the tender spot where she'd connected with the headboard.

How quickly she'd adjusted to having her new king-sized bed after she'd moved out on her own. A warm sense of nostalgia washed over her as she took a moment to enjoy the pale yellow walls, pinstriped curtains over blackout shades, and white furniture, trophies and ribbons on a high shelf—her old room at the farm. She flopped her arms out and touched the wall on one side, the edge of the mattress on the other. Her old bed. A double. *That*, she didn't miss at all.

She almost made it out of bed. *Yikes*. The floor was freezing. She'd have to rummage for slippers, and maybe a robe. She stumbled to the dresser to check the time on her cell phone. It was almost eleven, but the house was quiet, except for the soft music. With Joey and her siblings all grown and out of the house, the gift opening whirlwind was scheduled for later in the afternoon.

The aroma of fresh Columbian coffee drifting up the stairs stirred her taste buds, calling to her like blood to a vampire. The slippers would have to wait. She ran her fingers through her hair and followed the scent trail down the stairs all the way to the kitchen table, where a steaming mug stood waiting for her. She dropped on the chair, wrapped her hands around the coffee, and pulled it to her lips. "Thank you," she mumbled.

"You're welcome."

That was *not* her mother's voice. Her head shot up so fast she choked mid-swallow, nearly spewing out her coffee. She locked eyes with Fletch.

In that first surprised instant, she was struck by the beauty of his sharp cheek bones, thick dark hair and ocean-blue eyes framed with long, dark lashes. He looked stunning in a crisp white shirt and sharply pressed gray pants. She hadn't seen him in dress clothes before—ever.

"Where is everyone?" She managed to ask.

"Your parents were heading to church as I arrived."

"Church?" The intensity of his gaze was making her brain cells misfire.

"For the holiday service. It's Christmas Day."

"Oh." Deciding that caffeine was her only solution, she took another mouthful of the luscious brew and closed her eyes as she swallowed. Her father shared her commitment to coffee and could afford much better quality than she could at her house. She took another sip, this time appreciating the subtleties of the flavor as it flowed over her tongue. Finally, the caffeine started to hit her system.

Fletch's tone was deep and husky when he said, "You took my breath away, the very first time I saw you, Jo. And you still do, every single time I look at you."

That brought heat to more than her face and, against her will, dragged her eyes up from her coffee. She suddenly remembered she was sitting in the kitchen with bed head, puffy eyes and an unwashed face, wearing one of her oldest nighties. She jumped up, almost spilling her coffee, froze. Then, deciding it was hopeless, she dropped onto the chair. *Whatever.* Her cheeks burned but she wasn't going to hide away in her own home. Or former home, either.

"Thanks for coming, Fletch." After their call the night before, she hadn't expected him to show up.

He drew in an audible breath. "You're going to be the death of me one of these days, Jo."

His gravity didn't invite a smile, so she matched his serious tone. "Is that your way of saying you're going to help me talk to the families this afternoon?"

He pulled out a chair to sit across from her. "Despite my better judgement, yeah, I'll help you."

The tight strap that had wrapped itself around her chest, constricting every breath in or out, suddenly loosened its hold. She reached over and laid her hand on his. Even when his tensed, she held tight. "Thanks, Fletch. I'll feel better having you with me."

He was not looking happy about being there,

but the shadows playing in his eyes spoke of more than annoyance. He seemed troubled, and something more that she couldn't read.

"Are you still thinking about yesterday?" she asked.

~ ~ ~

Her question startled him but gave Fletch a good excuse, better than admitting how much she distracted him from everything else just by sitting there looking like she'd just tumbled out of bed. He wanted to tumble her right back in. "How did you know what I was thinking?"

"Maybe I'm starting to see what's underneath that tough skin of yours."

"Well-honed muscle?"

"That too, but I'm talking about that marshmallow heart of yours."

"Don't tell anyone. I'd lose my credibility."

"Cross my heart," she promised, with a twinkle in her eye.

It was like old times, sitting at the kitchen table, sharing a laugh. Except Joey had been less complicated back then. Or so he'd thought. Maybe he'd been too immature to recognize all the layers to her personality. He could see them now, and it made her an intriguing enigma. Tough cop, caring neighbor, enthusiastic lover, stubborn partner, loyal friend—

Her oval face had its own unique structure, shaped by her high curving cheekbones and the slender eyebrows arching over her gold-flecked eyes. Her strong, stubborn jaw was softened by that lush mouth. He wanted to reach out and touch her, hold her, kiss her. To wake up next to her every day. How could he possibly let her go again? Love was supposed to move mountains but could it build bridges and shore up the oceans keeping them apart? If they could barely work together effectively, how could he possibly hope to build a life with her? He'd been so certain as a teenager. But as a grown man? Especially one who had survived a tour through hell largely due to the rigor of military rules, whether those rules suit him or not? Were he and Joey an impossible match?

She tilted her head and looked at him, her expression solemn. "Fletch, you weren't to blame for what happened with those kids. Teens fight with their parents. They make poor decisions. That's just the way it is."

He'd followed the rules that time too and it almost cost two teenagers their lives. His gut knotted when he remembered how close to hypothermia the teens were when they finally found them huddled under the bridge. "Telling the mayor about Sammy set everything in motion, Jo. And *that* makes the whole thing my fault."

"And mine. I was fairly sure Sammy was the vandal even before I told you. Could I have done something sooner? Probably. Who knows if it would have changed anything?"

"You didn't have any proof."

"And you only had my word for it."

"But if I'd waited for you to get back to the office before telling Rufus—"

"Or if I'd told you where I was so you could run it by me before you told the chief—"

Joey was so sure of him and she was probably right about his part in sending the kids running. It had been his messed-up feelings about his relationship with her that had clouded his judgment. He was head over heels in love with her. Again. Yet, here she was, giving him what amounted to a sisterly pep talk. She had no idea what it was doing to him to have her sitting across from him just like she had when he'd fallen for her years before.

"At any point, any number of people could have done something differently, and it may, or may not, have made a difference. But you did everything you could to find those kids. No one is asking more of you than that...except you." She gave his hand a quick squeeze and let go. "We can *both* take some blame, as can their parents, and the kids themselves. The whole situation was a mess. But, yesterday, we also found them before they came to any harm. That counts for a lot." She leaned across the table and grabbed both his hands in her strong grip. Her voice was sure and earnest. "I hate to break it to you, Fletch, but sometimes you have to have a little faith that the rest of the world can take care of themselves without our help."

Unfortunately, he'd seen firsthand that, in some countries, they couldn't.

"Is that what you do?" he asked her.

"Hell, no. Never!"

Her answer didn't surprise him.

One thing at a time, his father always told him. If he could earn her trust at work, maybe they'd be able to sort out the personal side of things. "Jo, I didn't have to tell Rufus right away. I could have waited for you." He traced the grain of the oak with his fingertip. "I thought you hadn't come in because you were regretting the night before. Being with me. I let it get personal. For that I am sorry, Jo."

She flushed, and then shrugged it off. "It

happens, Fletch. We've both been off our game the last few days. Anyway, I'd better get ready. Make yourself at home." Then she stopped and looked around the kitchen. "Oh, I guess you already have. Wanna throw on some toast for me in about ten minutes?" With a smile and a wink she left.

~~~

It wasn't until she had showered and gone to her room to get dressed that she thought about the dress code for a Frost family Christmas dinner. She'd arrived with the two teenagers the night before still in her uniform, and had pulled an old flannel nightie out of her dresser to sleep in. Normally, she didn't give much thought to what she wore. Mostly jeans, add a nice blouse and a spritz of perfume when she had to dress up. But Christmas Day was a big deal in the Frost household and turning up in sweats wasn't going to cut it. And she had the intervention with the Lincolns and the Belmonts as well. She didn't want to give the impression it was official police business by showing up in her uniform. Her mother's dresses would be indecently short on her, so she didn't have many options. With a grimace, she yanked open the closet doors to scope out the remnants she'd left behind when she moved. Unfortunately they consisted of a few truly hideous bridesmaids dresses she'd worn over the years. Pushing those aside, she found one last possibility.

Sliding off the protective, clear plastic, her heart gave a lurch when she recognized the cobalt jersey wrap-dress that she'd worn to a year-end high school dance. It was her first grownup dress, although it covered her from head to mid-calf even covering her arms to the wrist. The material flowed over her body like a whispering stream and exposed a flash of leg when she moved. With her mother's help, she'd worn her hair swept to one side to cascade over her shoulder almost to her waist like a waterfall, and just a little bit of makeup. *Less is more, my darling*, her mother had instructed as she helped her get ready.

With a heavy sigh, she slipped it off the hanger and tried it on. A twirl in front of the full-length mirror, confirmed it still fit well enough thanks to the forgiving style of the dress. She may not have gained weight since high school, but some of it had relocated to give her a more mature figure. The matching heels were still buried in the corner of the closet where she'd tossed them years ago. Feeling just as self-conscious this time, she made her way downstairs.

One final stop in the hall to make sure her dress was crossing her chest at a discreet point and she promised herself she'd stop fussing with it. Leaving her hair down in loose waves was her attempt to draw attention away from her cleavage. She double knotted the bow of the self-tie belt so she wouldn't have to worry about it loosening during the afternoon. At times like this, Joey wished she had more of her mother's natural sophistication. She entered the living room.

"You looked beautiful in that dress the first time I saw you in it, but my memory sure didn't do you justice. You look spectacular." Fletch was slowly rising from her father's favorite chair in the corner. He'd apparently been reading a book, which had fallen unnoticed to the floor at his feet. There was no mistaking the hunger in his eyes.

Joey was torn between self-consciousness, and the urge to throw her chest out and lick her lips for good measure, just to make him see what he'd been missing. "I didn't stop to pick up clothes from home on my way here last night with the kids. This is one from years ago that I found in the closet. I can't remember how long I've had it." She was lying, of course. She knew exactly when she'd worn it. It had only been that one time, about a month after he'd kissed her. She was surprised *he* remembered the dress.

"It was the very last time I saw you. At the end of my senior year. You were at the dance with Eric Wedge, and I spent the whole night wanting to wring his neck. I left town a few days later to meet up with my parents."

That wasn't her recollection. She had accepted the date with Wedge, which wasn't fair to him. Yet, he'd been a good friend to her that night, treating her with kid gloves as if he knew her heart was fragile. And she was sure Fletch hadn't so much as glanced at her. "You already had a date with a cheerleader, as I recall. What were you doing looking at me?"

"Every guy in the hall was looking at you that night, sweetheart."

Hearing that did nothing to calm her nerves but it was time to change the subject. She sank onto the sofa and watched the small hand of the clock move. Her foot twitched as it jumped forward to the next number.

"The Belmonts and Lincolns should be here by now. I wonder what's keeping them."

"The Belmonts have small children to get dressed and out the door as well as themselves. That's no easy task."

"What time is your Aunt Elle expecting you for dinner?"

"She goes to Burlington to spend the holiday with her niece's family."

Joey stared at him, stricken. "Were you supposed to go with her? You didn't have to stay for this."

"No, it's the other side of the family. They offered, of course, but I said I had other plans."

His face was blank, but Joey wondered if she'd had anything to do with those plans. Between the investigations, and the fact she was the only single person in her family this year, she'd avoided thinking about the holiday. She'd had a moment of hope when they'd spent the evening together but everything fell apart the very next morning. That one night had proven she had no resistance when she let Fletch get too close. Heat crept into her cheeks. "I assumed you were spending the day with her. I'm sorry. I didn't even think to check. Why don't you stay here for dinner?"

The doorbell interrupted them before he responded.

She stood, tugged her dress into place, and licked her lips. Fletch raised his eyebrows, but said nothing.

It was Mr. and Mrs. Lincoln. Both were well dressed but Emerson Lincoln was more subdued than she'd ever seen him. She barely had time to take their coats, before the doorbell rang again. This time Joey opened the door to three little munchkins, who immediately pulled off their hats and mittens and pushed through her legs. Verna Belmont grabbed the twins, as Oliver swept the toddler up in his arms. The fourth sibling, hanging back behind her mother, was unmistakeably Ivy's little sister, Anna. All were dressed in their clean and pressed Sunday best.

Joey gave Verna a hug and scanned Oliver. His eyes were alert and clear, and his breath was fresh when he leaned in to shake her hand. He was sober.

She picked up the kids' winter things from the floor as Sylvia Frost appeared to welcome the guests. "Happy Holidays. Come in. Why don't I take the little ones into the kitchen for cookies and milk, while the adults get settled in the living room?"

Harold Frost, Fletch and the Lincolns stood as the Belmonts entered the room, and an awkward silence hung in the air. Joey looked at Fletch who immediately settled into his seat and left her to fend for herself. Some partner he was. Well, she would do just that. She didn't need her partner for this.

"Please sit down, Mr. and Mrs. Belmont. Mr. and Mrs. Lincoln."

There was a general rustle of activity as everyone found a seat. Her father and mother discreetly stepped out of the room. Joey's skin twitched with the tension in the room. Or was she the only one buzzing with jangled nerves? "Most importantly, I wanted to reassure you all that Sammy and Ivy are fine, fully recovered from their adventure yesterday."

All the parents spoke at once, asking where they were and demanding they be present. Joey raised her hands to calm them.

"The second thing I want to make perfectly clear is that I'm not here in any official capacity. The kids just asked me to help you understand why they acted the way they did. They know how much I care about them both. I've lived in Carol Falls my whole life and I want to do everything I can to make sure the people who live here are safe and secure. This town is home to all of us."

She gave a head nod to her silent partner sitting in the corner. "And Fletch is simply a caring friend." She put emphasis on the 'caring' so he'd know his role.

First she spoke to the Lincolns. "I've known Sammy since he was a toddler. Changed his diapers, helped him with his school work, and listened to his girl troubles." Mrs. Lincoln smiled and nodded. Joey wasn't sure the mayor knew that history.

She turned to the Belmonts. "I wish I could have known Ivy as long, but I think I've gotten a good sense of her character over the last little while. I've seen how she put her own schooling on hold when she felt her younger siblings needed her." She threw a stern look at Mr. Belmont when she added, "And I've seen her defend her father to protect him from the fallout of his own behavior."

The senior Belmont sank into his chair, but didn't look away. He deserved points for that. "Did you know Sammy was tutoring Ivy so she wouldn't fall behind in her studies?"

She didn't wait for an answer. "And I think Ivy tried to talk Sammy into coming to me about the vandalism?" It was what she thought she'd seen them talking about several days before. "They just ran out of time." She avoided eye contact with Fletch. That quarrel was behind them.

All four parents looked at each other. Clearly none of them fully knew what was going on between their teens. Both fathers slumped forward in the seats, their heads bowed and their hands clasped between their knees. Someone sniffed, but

Joey couldn't tell who was fighting the tears.

Oliver Belmont spoke up first. He stood and went over to the mayor, who immediately bolted up from his chair as well.

Fletch moved, but Joey signaled him to stay put and held her breath.

Oliver's voice was gruff with emotion, but strong with conviction. "I know it won't undo the things I've done to you and your wife, and I'm ready to accept the consequences of my actions. But, I want to say how very sorry I am for using you as an excuse for my own problems. I've already apologized to my wife for my unacceptable behavior, and I'm lucky enough to have her forgiveness. I don't deserve the same from you, but I beg you not to punish my wife or my daughter for my bad judgment."

The mayor was silent as his wife rose to step in front of her husband. She hugged Oliver. "Mr. Belmont, we understand the stress of your situation and certainly accept your apology. Emotions can run high this time of year." She glared at her husband who for once seemed to be deferring to his wife. "My husband and I discussed the situation last night and were planning to approach Verna about coming back to us, if she'll accept us again as her client." She dropped her chin and locked eyes with her husband. He walked over to Verna and took her hand. "I overreacted, Verna. I'd just heard that Sammy was in trouble and I took it out on you. It was unforgiveable and undeserved. I sincerely apologize."

Verna's eyes watered. "Mr. Lincoln. Children are so difficult to raise, it's a wonder we don't all just lose our minds completely."

Joey's throat was so tight she could hardly get the rest of the words out, but she felt hope take root and, shoved her hands behind her back so no one would see when she crossed her fingers.

"What I do know about those two wonderful teens is that they have warm and loving hearts that were almost broken by the circumstances they found themselves in." She looked around the room and caught Fletch watching her with an intensity she couldn't read and it frightened her. She turned away from him when the floor boards creaked behind her. Everyone looked up. Sammy and Ivy stood in the archway between the living and dining room, where Joey had told them they could wait and listen. She had left the decision with them, whether they would join their parents. It looked like Joey was getting her Christmas wish. "Fortunately, as their parents, you raised them to be resilient and forgiving."

Sammy moved into the room first. Ivy followed, holding the sleeping baby over her shoulder and gently patting her diapered bottom. To comfort herself as much as the infant, Joey suspected. Did that give more credence to the suspicion Ivy might be the child's mother? Were they about to confess to being baby Holly's parents?

Without taking her eyes off her family, Ivy handed the baby to Fletch, who took the bundle with practiced care. The tiny head disappeared in the palm of his strong hand and he gently settled her along his forearm. Joey tore her gaze away from the curious sight to watch Verna envelop Ivy in a full body embrace. Her father then wrapped his arms around both of his women.

Sammy tentatively approached his parents, still not sure of his father's reception. The mayor seemed mesmerized by the boy, paralyzed, as if seeing the clone of his younger self for the first time. Then he opened his arms and grabbed his son in a bear hug. Joey could hear muffled words but stepped out of range to allow them privacy. Fletch was suddenly at her side, with the sleeping baby still on his arm, and leaned into her ear. "Did I miss the line in your job description about effective meddling?" he whispered, his voice even.

Seeing the success of her efforts, Joey was glad she'd meddled. She kept her voice low so the others in the room wouldn't hear their conversation. "It didn't preclude it, when I'm not on duty. Fletch, I do get what you're saying though. I almost slipped up and questioned the kids on the drive here last night. But I heard you nagging in my head, so I stopped."

"I guess I'm glad to hear that, although I have no idea what you're talking about."

"About baby Holly." She stroked the infant stirring in his arms. "We need to ask Sammy and Ivy if she's theirs."

"You were going to ask them without the parents present." He made it a statement. She'd expected him to get mad again. Or at least be surprised. But he took it in stride.

"Thought about it. But I didn't." She eased the tiny bundle from his arms, trying not to wake her. "However, we do have the parents here now."

Joey cleared her throat to get their attention. When she had it, she said, "There is one more small matter I'd like to clear up—"

She looked at both sets of parents in turn.

"—if the parents are okay with it."

Then she turned to Sammy and Ivy. "Could I

ask you guys one other question? You don't have to tell me if you don't want to. Or if you would rather talk to your parents first."

That would never pass for reading them their rights. Joey looked at Fletch and saw that he had the same thought, but he didn't stop her.

"Fletch. You don't have to be here if you want to leave."

He gave her the same intense look as before, as if he was tunneling into her soul to see if she was worth the trouble she was causing him. Whatever he saw satisfied him.

"I'll stay," he said.

The two teens were sitting together on the love seat, both leaning forward. She turned away from them and kept her voice so low only the parents could hear. "I need to ask the kids about a pregnancy. Is that okay?"

Shock, confusion, and denial crossed the faces of all four adults. She didn't pressure them. The color drained out of Mrs. Lincoln's face. Joey thought Verna might faint. The idea of her child having a child must be terrifying. The mayor found his voice first. "We can stop you at any point, right?"

"Absolutely. That would be a prudent thing to do and I'll go slowly."

While she settled the infant over her shoulder, Fletch positioned a chair so Joey could sit in front of the two teens. "Now guys, take your time to answer, okay."

Two heads nodded. Joey struggled with the best way to phrase things. With the baby in her arms, rocking was a natural reflex. "Did your running away have anything to do with baby

Holly?"

She thought she'd been fairly smooth, but apparently she'd caught the teens completely off guard. Their eyes stretched so wide, she saw the flash of white. Then they looked at each other, before dropping their faces into their hands and starting to shake. Joey felt a stab of panic. Ivy pulled herself up and, seeing the glisten of tears on her cheeks, Joey opened her mouth to try damage control...and then realized the two kids were laughing. Ivy dissolved into another fit of giggles, while Sammy grabbed his chest trying to catch his breath.

"Holy crap, Joey. Ivy and I haven't even—"

Suddenly, Sammy's cheeks reddened as he must've remembered their parents were in the room.

The idea was a sobering thought for Ivy as well and she immediately settled down. "Does everyone think that's why we ran away? We'd never desert a helpless baby, especially if it was our own," she said.

Someone sucked in a breath behind her. Both of the teenagers' faces had suddenly taken on a maturity well beyond their years. Joey felt a weight slip from her shoulders. "I have to think of every possibility, but I doubt it's even crossed anyone else's mind, Ivy. I just wanted to make sure we had it covered in case it came up officially."

There was a brief silence as everyone in the room considered the seriousness of the situation and what it might have meant for the two young people in the room.

"Then who *is* the mother of baby Holly?" asked Mrs. Lincoln, speaking for all of them.

As if to express her own frustration, the tiny girl chose that moment to cry. Joey stood up to rock her and studied the circle of people around her. Ivy and Sammy looked calm, but the adults were a different story. The mayor's face was flushed, he really needed to get his blood pressure checked, and his wife was looking at the baby with the doting sadness Joey had seen from all the women at the coffee club. Oliver Belmont looked like he needed a drink, but Verna's frail body seemed to cave in on itself as she wrung her hands.

And in that moment, Joey knew. But proving it would be a completely different matter. She shifted Holly to cradle her in her arms, looking at the tiny face, and wishing babies looked more like their parents right from birth. Her instincts were quaking and she had seconds to decide whether to act on them. If she confirmed the identity, both mother and child could be taken away from their town. From her town. If she didn't do something now, the baby could eventually be adopted by a family in another town or even a different state, and be forever lost to her birth mother and her home town. The tornado of thoughts whirled until her head hurt. Sometimes, faith needed a little boost.

"I'm not having any luck quieting her, Verna. Would you mind giving it a try?" With that said, Joey held out the fussing infant.

Verna hesitated for an instant, and then as if her arms were tugged by invisible strings, she reached out and cradled the baby against her chest. The baby settled immediately, while her mother melted into heartrending sobs, "My poor baby. My sweet little girl."

Joey put a gentle arm around Verna's waist and guided her out of the room. She heard Oliver

Belmont following behind them, saying in a pained whisper, "You gave away our baby? Was I so bad—?"

Sylvia Frost intercepted them in the hallway and quietly convinced Oliver to give his wife a little time and space, as Joey pushed open the door to her father's study. The room was lined with bookshelves, and in the center was a heavy carved desk, handed down through several generations of Frost men. It was where she'd had all her serious talks with her father, where he doled out sage advice to his children, and planned their futures. It seemed like the best place to interview Verna. Joey settled the distraught woman in a wing-backed chair beside the gas fireplace for warmth. Then she crouched at eye level, and said, "Verna, I can only help you if I know why you left your baby in the manger."

Chapter Twelve

Fletch struggled to keep his face expressionless as he handed a glass of water to the Belmont woman and then quietly took up a position against the far wall nearest the door. He wanted to be unobtrusive, but close at hand if Joey needed him.

Joey had positioned Verna beside a fireplace at the far end of the room. He watched silently, as Joey tucked a pillow under the mother's arm to support her babe more comfortably. His thoughts were in chaos. How had Joey known Verna was the mother? What was going to happen to this poor woman now? And what about the rest of those children? Their father was making an effort but had a long, hard journey ahead of him.

The baby whimpered once but stopped as soon as Verna swayed her upper body to some internal rhythm that only a mother knows. Fletch was glad he wasn't going to be the one taking the baby away from her. Joey would handle it much better than he ever could. This whole incident had given him new respect for Joey's strength in dealing with her people. She knew what they needed her to do, and then she did it, without having to ask or think. It was all instinct with her. Like the type of hunches other officers had about criminal behavior. At this point, he really didn't know if Joey's actions would make things better or worse for the Belmonts. She'd solved the puzzle of the abandoned baby, but now the entire Belmont family might fall apart. It was like watching a train wreck and, just like in Afghanistan, there was nothing he could do to stop it or protect any of those children. For once, he just wanted to help instead of standing by being useless. At least Joey was trying her damnedest. All he'd done so far was spout rules and regulations, and stand in her way. He scrubbed his face with his free hand.

Joey left the Belmont woman to join him near the wall. "We need to know what happened so we can help her. Fletch, she's been through too much," she whispered close to his ear.

He breathed in the light floral scent he associated with Joey. When she stepped away, he was stuck anew with her rare kind of beauty, like a hand-painted portrait. Her honeyed-ivory skin glowed with assurance as her eyes begged him to help her do the right thing. But he was no King Solomon. He wasn't trained to choose between following the law or helping a mother and child in trouble. His gut knotted.

Joey had grown into an amazingly strong, independent woman who still took his breath away. And since it *was* Joey asking, how far outside the line was he prepared to go for her? He closed his eyes for a moment. It didn't even take that long to decide. He'd go as far as it took. Because he loved her too much to do anything else. He was about to ask her what she needed him to do this time, when the answer hit him, like a slap in the face. Joey was asking him to trust her.

He had no reservations when he responded, "It's okay. I'll follow your lead. But promise me that, eventually, you'll tell me how you figured this one out."

They pulled two chairs over to where Verna sat, rocking and humming. The baby made a small mewling sound, obviously content to be in her mother's arms at last. Fletch tried to make himself invisible, thinking it was better to let the women talk, but he worried Verna had already slipped too far under the stress.

She surprised him. "What will happen to me now?"

If Joey was surprised or uncertain, it didn't show. She kept her voice soft and even. "We were just trying to figure that out. Verna, I want to be upfront with you. It's against the law to abandon a baby."

The older woman nodded sadly and stroked the little one's head with her hand. "I know."

"Can you tell me what happened?"

"My husband is a good man and we've tried to do right by our family. But, with Ollie out of work, I'm barely caring for my other babies." Her voice dropped to a whisper. "When I found out I was pregnant again, my husband's drinking was getting worse. I didn't want to add to his worries by telling him we were going to have another mouth to feed. I just prayed that he'd get a job soon, and things would work out."

She met Joey's gaze and gave her a watery smile. "I was thrilled when your brother gave Ollie that job at the farm, but then his drinking got him fired. And after that, everything went from bad to worse. He started blaming Mayor Lincoln for all his troubles and taking out his frustrations on me and Ivy." Verna flushed with shame as if it was somehow her fault, and her problem to fix. Joey reached out to squeeze the woman's free hand in silent support.

"The baby wasn't due until January so I hid it under loose clothing and hoped Ollie might settle down again after Christmas. But she came early."

Verna paused, voice shaking, eyes swimming. "I was so afraid the added stress and financial burden might tip Ollie over the edge. He's not himself anymore." Her voice dropped so low, and she bowed her head so Fletch wasn't sure he heard her say, "I was just afraid he'd hurt the baby."

The memory of the solemn faces of the children standing silently in the hall of the home was etched in Fletch's brain. It was their job as officers of the law to help this woman and her family. Then, he remembered something he'd read recently at the police station. His mind raced but he spoke gently, not wanting to frighten the woman despite his good intentions. "Verna, where did you give birth?"

"At home. Ivy was out when I felt the labor pains. I sent the children next door for a few hours. I only do that in an emergency because Mrs. White is getting too old to chase little ones around. This one's my sixth child so everything happened so fast."

"And then you went directly to the Frost farm?"

Joey was looking at him, obviously not following his line of questions.

When Verna nodded, a small ray of hope lay

within his grasp. He turned to Joey to explain. "I reviewed the Vermont Statutes in case anything had changed while I was overseas." He didn't tell her it was his aggravation with her constant bending of the law that had driven him to question it and his own sanity. "There's an exception to the Abandonment of Baby law."

Joey's brow creased in confusion. "But Verna didn't hand baby Holly over to a Safe Haven."

He was still working it out in his mind, but the pieces seemed to fit. "I think we could say she did. Vermont is one of the states that recognizes emergency crews and law enforcement agents as safe havens who can accept infants. Verna brought her baby all the way to Frost farm, right after giving birth the night of Frosty Frolics."

Joey caught his argument and turned to Verna. "And you would only do that because you knew the chief of police was there, as well as every other medical professional in town, and just about anyone else you might need."

Joey looked at Fletch, her cheeks flushed with excitement. "What about the rest of the requirements?"

Fletch rubbed his temples trying to remember what he'd read. "The safe haven provider is required to accept emergency protective custody of the infant and to provide any immediate medical care the infant may require."

He looked at her as she nodded like a bobble doll. "They did that. Garret told me Chief Slayton and the choir director, who's a registered nurse, took a good look at the baby up at the house. She was absolutely fine, Fletch. The nurse told them she was perfectly healthy."

Fletch tensed and pinned Joey with his stare. "This is the last piece but it's really important. Did you report the incident to family service? Please tell me you did, Jo."

Color rose in her cheeks, and in that instant he wanted to shake her. Just this once, couldn't she have followed the rules?

"I didn't, Fletch. I was away on a course that night. The case went to Wedge. *He* notified family services. Fletch, Wedge caught the case instead of me." A tear ran down her cheek. "It was Wedge. He made the call and documented it in his report. He's a stickler for procedures and details. Just like you." Joey grabbed Fletch's hands with both of hers. They locked eyes and he felt the adrenalin, energy and something more flow between them. "It's a stretch, Fletch."

He nodded. "A big stretch."

"You're okay with it though?" she asked.

He searched his heart for some sign of discomfort about what they were doing. All he found was profound satisfaction,...and peace,...and love. All things a man could search for his whole life, and never find. He looked at his partner, and the knot in his gut finally relaxed. "My conscience is clear, Jo. And I think you can convince the State, and family services, because you can get the backing of your parents, the mayor, the ladies' coffee club, and the entire community behind you." They'd done it. Together, he and Joey had finally managed to combine strengths and minds to really help this family.

A smile spread across Joey's lovely face, sending a flush across her cheeks and igniting sparks in her eyes.

A small voice broke in, "I don't understand."

They'd completely forgotten that Verna was sitting beside them with a personal stake in their discussion.

"Am I under arrest?"

Joey hugged her, baby and all. "No, Verna, you are not under arrest. As far as we're concerned, you turned baby Holly over to a Safe Haven as legally allowed under the law in the State of Vermont."

Verna burst into tears again. "Thank you, Officer Joey. Thank you so much for saving my family."

"It wasn't me, Verna. You need to thank Officer Fletcher for knowing the law to the letter."

"Thank you, too, Officer. Thank you for caring about us." Verna wrapped her cold fingers around his forearm and he covered her hand with his own, wishing he could solve the rest of her problems too. "What will happen to my baby now?"

"We can't promise anything, Mrs. Belmont," Fletch cautioned, catching Joey's eye as he did. They still needed to manage expectations and be prepared, in case things didn't go as expected. "But we're very optimistic. We're betting that family services will want to let the good people of Carol Falls help you get your family back together and solidly on its feet again."

Verna's body straightened and her face suddenly exuded strength from somewhere deep inside. She looked young and alive for the first time since he'd met her.

Joey stood and helped Verna rise without jostling the baby. "I think you and Holly need a nap before dinner, Verna. Mom put fresh sheets on the bed at the top of the stairs."

Sylvia appeared on cue to provide the needed support.

Joey closed the door behind them and flopped onto the sofa, and let her head drop back.

Fletch sank down beside her. His head was reeling from everything he'd witnessed in the last couple of hours.

"How did you know it was Mrs. Belmont, Jo?"

She rolled her head to the side. "I'd like to say it was dogged investigation, but I'd be lying. Everything seemed to point to Ivy Belmont. And there, the only hard evidence linking to the Belmont household was the baby quilt Holly was wrapped in when she was found. I noticed that the other Belmont kids had similar ones when we were at the house—the little guy was dragging one around, and then there was one on the girls' twin beds yesterday. I'd spent hours staring at the photo of Holly's but it wasn't the same as seeing the genuine article or I might have clicked to it sooner."

"So you were fishing by interviewing Sammy and Ivy?"

"Not completely. I had to eliminate them. But I wasn't surprised at their reaction."

"Why didn't you just bring Ivy and her parents in to question them sooner?" Joey could have solved the case almost as soon as it was transferred over to her, and come out looking like a star.

"I just couldn't get my head around it being Ivy, knowing how responsible she was with the younger kids, her father, her schooling. She's so mature, well beyond her years. And the same with Sammy. I couldn't see those two leaving the child when they ran away yesterday. Did you know they were running away to get married? I think that's what they would have done if they got pregnant. They're romantics."

Of course, Joey wouldn't put career advancement ahead of the interests of her town. She wouldn't have wanted to cause the Belmonts any more discomfort by hauling them in for questioning in case she was wrong. Fletch said, "That was no accident, handing the baby to Verna, was it? How did you know?" Fletch's respect for Joey's skills was on a straight vertical climb.

"It was mostly something about her reaction when the baby cried while she was standing right there. It was there in her face, her eyes. In that instant, other bits and pieces just clicked in my mind. Verna's desperate need to take the baby from me, to soothe her, was almost tangible. Only the mother would feel that. Other than that, it was a hunch. She's been around her own baby for weeks but not able to hold her. It must have been horrible for her. So I gave her the chance."

"Knowing it would break her."

"Not break her, Fletch. She was broken from the moment she left her baby in the manger. Having Holly *back* will make her whole again."

He let out a low whistle. "She gave birth by herself, rounded up her other children to get them to a sitter, then bundled up her newborn and drove to your parents' farm to make sure the child was left in a safe place."

"Walked." Joey said.

He turned his head to look at her. "Huh? Walked?"

"Verna doesn't drive. She must have bundled up her new born and *walked* up to the farm from her place to put her baby safely in the manger."

"She's so fragile looking. I thought she was a weak woman."

Joey laughed. "No such thing."

Fletch had come to the same conclusion about Joey, too.

The front door banged open and a young boy's voice echoed through the house. "Grandma? Where are you, Grandma?"

"No running in the house, son," boomed a more mature male voice.

"That's my nephew, Duncan. Garret and his new girlfriend must be here," Joey said. They both started to laugh and pushed up from their seat. "Let the holiday begin," they said in unison.

After slowing his five year old son to a walk in search of his grandmother, Garret Frost introduced Fletch to his public relations manager, Lily Parker. The way the guy was devouring Lily with his eyes, left no doubt they had more than a working relationship.

"Fletch. Glad to see you're back. Are you staying this time?" Garret asked, pointedly. Did every member of the Frost family have a memory like a steel trap? Before Fletch had time to respond, the second Frost brother, Jimmy, arrived with his high school sweetheart, April Rochester, and her ten year old son, Marcus. He and Jimmy gave each other a guy hug and started talking football as if no time had passed. In the back of his mind, Fletch considered asking his buddy for his secret to romance, but in his heart, Fletch figured he'd already failed his mission to win Joey's heart. He could blame age and inexperience when he left her at eighteen. He had no excuse this time. He'd been so intent on trying to make *her* trust his judgment, he'd forgotten *he* had to trust hers. Aunt Elle told him relationships that were meant to be, worked out against all odds, but she'd also taught him that without trust, there could be no relationship.

When Jimmy moved on to show off his new family to the rest of the guests, Fletch wandered over to the archway leading to the hall. He stuck his hands in his pockets and leaned against the doorjamb, trying to memorize every detail of the scene playing out in front of him. It was the perfect picture of a family Christmas—the type he'd always wished for, but could never have.

Joey was in her element, wrapped in that dynamite dress, floating from person to person, making the Belmonts feel welcome, laughing with her brothers, scooping up her nephew to squeals of laughter. An amazing woman and an accomplished police officer. She would always be a bit unconventional by his military standards, but her special touch with the people she served, her people, was a big part of what made her so good at her job. She'd shown him a trick or two while he watched her working her cases. He was confident she had learned to recognize the fine line between the law and justice. He didn't regret returning to Carol Falls, though, even if all he left with was the memory of this Christmas moment. Joey was glowing with love for those around her, optimism for the future no matter what obstacles lay in her path in the present, and her happiness with her life. That was really what he'd wanted most for her all along. It would be unfair of him to ask her to leave all that to be with him in Boston. His childhood and career made it easier for him to accept loneliness and move on. It was the life he'd been given, or maybe it was what he'd chosen. Her life was here in

Carol Falls. Without him.

He straightened and, with a final glance around the room, he slipped out to the hallway thinking he should show up early for the job in Boston. It wouldn't take him long to gather his few belongings, stop by the station to make the call to Rufus and clear out his desk. He had a small present for Joey, but he could leave it on her desk and hit the road tonight. The best thing he could do for Joey now was get his butt out of her way and tell her boss he was a jackass for not seeing that he already had the best candidate for deputy chief in his own ranks.

He thought he could slip out the door unnoticed but he was caught with his hand on the doorknob.

"Hey, mister. Where'ya'goin'? We haven't eaten yet." A small boy stared up at him with the Frosts' hazel eyes.

The little boy saw the world in such simple terms, Fletch envied him. He kept his answer simple. "It's time for me to go now."

"It's not polite to leave without saying goodbye."

Such a smart kid, too. He dropped into a crouch so they could talk man to man. "It gets complicated at Christmas. In most cases you thank the hostess when you leave, but right now it would be worse to interrupt everyone while they're all talking to each other."

The kid looked into the room and saw the truth of what he said. "I guess so. Dad always says it's rude for me to interrupt adults."

Fletch tried to look like a wise adult. "Don't worry. It takes a while to get the hang of all the rules." He reached into his pocket and passed the boy a small wrapped box. "But could I ask you to do me a very special favor?"

~~~

Joey hadn't seen Fletch in almost an hour. She thought he'd been with her brother, but Jimmy had wandered through the living room five minutes before to hug his new wife. She caught him before he was out of earshot. "Have you seen Fletch, Jimmy?"

"Not in a while, Sis."

The chatter and laughter suddenly faded as she scanned the room looking for his dark hair above the crowd in the room. Duncan tugged on her dress to get her attention. "He had to go but he left you a present."

Joey's stomach clenched as she took the pretty gift from her nephew. *Why didn't he wait to give it to me himself?*

Duncan suddenly jumped up and down in excitement. "Oh, and he gave me a message for you too. He said to tell you—"

The little boy squeezed his eyes shut. "You are a great police officer, and—"

He sucked a deep breath in.

"—he's *soooo* proud of you." The beautiful, innocent eyes opened and his lips stretched into a huge smile. He vibrated with excitement as she slipped off the ribbon.

Inside the box, wrapped in white tissue paper, was a delicate porcelain ornament of a young couple. A pretty blonde girl was holding hands with a handsome dark haired boy—who was carrying two pairs of skates in his other hand.

Joey pressed a hand to her mouth ready to stifle the sob if it broke free. Joy, panic and then anger swept through her, snapping her out of her shock at seeing the reminder of their shared past. Oh no. You are *not* doing this to me again.

Joey dropped into a squat in front of her beloved nephew, took his flushed face in her hands, and kissed first one cheek, then the other. "You are a fabulous messenger, Duncan. Now can you give one to Grandma for me?"

He nodded enthusiastically, and readied himself to memorize her words. Her love for this little boy overwhelmed her, flooding her eyes with tears. "Tell her, I'll be back in time for dinner." Giving the boy one more kiss for the road, Joey grabbed her jacket and boots, and raced out the door.

Chapter Thirteen

Fletch had to pull over after he passed through the red covered bridge that marked the town limits. He focused on the jagged mountain peaks cutting into the low-lying clouds as he rubbed his chest to ease the ache under his rib cage. He was doing the right thing, getting out of Joey's way for the job. Rufus had taken his recommendation that Joey was ready for the promotion now. And Fletch hadn't lied when he told the chief that, after his experience with the Carol Falls PD, he'd be bringing more heart to his detective work in Boston. Except, his heart wasn't going to Boston. It was going to remain right where he'd left it when he was eighteen—in Carol Falls, with Joey.

He got out of the car to look out over the town one last time. If he believed in Christmas miracles, he would wish for one more chance to tell Joey he loved her, without tangling things up with the job and rules and all the other stuff that seemed to get in their way. He just wanted to be with her, without any conditions, for as long as she wanted him. But it was what *she* wanted that mattered, and that was her town, her job and her family. He was caught up in his thoughts, when he noticed the flashing lights approaching the bridge from town. There were no other cars in sight of the bridge—no surprise since it was Christmas Day. Could be a CheckStop to make sure no one tried to drive home on the highway after having too much holiday cheer. Probably wondering what he was doing standing there. He leaned into his car for the registration, assuming the officer would be asking for it.

"Where are you headed in such a hurry? You have to check in with the local police before you leave town, you know?" Joey walked up to him and stood so close, he was effectively pinned against his car. On her breath, he could smell the sweetness of a shortbread cookie she must have snatched on the way out the door. He could see that behind the humor, there was sadness. Her voice was husky with emotion. "Fletch, were you really going to leave me without so much as a good-bye?"

She grabbed his collar and kissed him on the mouth with so much passion he almost lost his balance. Then she released him, and stepped away. Her eyes glistened, so he reached up to cup her cheek. "Sweetheart, I talked to Rufus. The job is yours. You should have been given it in the first place."

She straightened. Her arms dropped to her side. "The position is only contract anyway so that isn't important. I just thought there'd be more time before you had to leave." She didn't pose it as a question. It struck him like a shot to the head. She's heard about the job in Boston and believed he'd planned to leave all along. And based on his history, he supposed she was right. But he could be a man about it.

"Jo, the deputy chief position is permanent. *I* was the one who asked for it to be a temporary contract."

"Why would you do that?" The pain in her eyes tore him apart.

"Because I knew I couldn't stay in Carol Falls if things didn't work out with you."

"I don't understand. What did I have to do with it?"

"I took a detective job with the Boston PD and, at first I thought I would ask you to come with me. I only took the job with Rufus as an excuse to come here to find you and give you time to decide if that was what *you* wanted...to be with me.

She was staring at him, unblinking, her lips parted. He wanted to kiss those lips, badly, but he had to finish this the right way for once.

"You came here for *me*?" Her hand was shaking, as she brushed away a strand of hair from her forehead.

"Jo, I told you the truth when I said I didn't know you were a cop. But, after seeing you here in Carol Falls, I realize this is where you belong. And, I'm also telling you the truth that I can't stay in Carol Falls to watch you fall in love with someone else, and marry him, and have a family with him."

Her tongue peeked out long enough to wet her lips, then disappeared. "Why on earth would I do that when I love *you*? And, for your information, I'd consider leaving my job, and any other option, to be with you." She moved in until they stood so close the steam from their breath joined to form a single soft white cloud. "But, Fletch, we can't work anything out if *you* walk away."

She was daring him to deny the words of wisdom he'd given to her earlier. Finally, he opened his arms and his heart to her. He brushed his lips against her neck and whispered a promise. "I have been in love with you since the day we met, and I promise you I'll stay with you for as long as you want me in your life."

"Then you'd better be prepared to lay down some roots this time, Fletch." She showed him the beautiful ornament she'd been cradling in her hand. "I didn't believe that night meant anything to you until I opened this." She gently closed her fingers around the treasured gift and clutched it to her heart. "I'm not letting you go this time."

She pressed her face into his neck, and his heart hitched. Her cheek was damp. He swore as he kissed her temple and held her close. They didn't need words again until Joey tilted her head, and without loosening her hold on him, she said, "Do I still get the Deputy job?"

"Sure, I can report to you this time." He tried to hide his grimace. Being partners on the job was going to take a little more work.

~~~

Joey wanted to stay tucked against his chest forever, but Christmas dinner was waiting for them at the farmhouse. As they parted to turn their cars around, her cell phone rang. Fletch waited while she answered it.

"Buddy is ready to come home for Christmas too," she said, her heart swelling with relief and happiness.

"Did you know she was a female?" he asked.

This time Joey was ready with her excuse for not noticing the dog's gender. She shrugged nonchalantly. "Sure. Buddy is short for Rosebud."

Fletch looked unconvinced. "Oh. Do you want me to pick her up so you can get back to help your mother? Should I bring her to your place or your parents'?"

"She's probably upset so I don't want her alone at my house. Let's bring her to the farm and we can take her home with us after dinner."

A grinned tugged at his mouth before she realized she'd assumed Fletch was coming home with her.

He didn't argue. "Sounds good. I'll meet you at the farm." He lightly brushed his lips across hers.

She closed her eyes and savored the warmth and softness. The pressure increased as his arm came around her waist, pulling her closer. She burrowed inside his unzipped jacket so she could listen to his strong, steady heartbeat. She could trust Fletch, even if she pushed too far, or too fast. He was the kind of guy you could build a home with and know the foundation was solid.

Chapter Fourteen

Joey stood watching everyone, rocking on her heels and hugging herself, afraid she might explode with joy. Duncan started a game of tag, running after the young Belmont twins. The house filled with noise and laughter. Oliver Belmont had his arm around Verna who had yet to put down baby Holly. Her husband had been filling his glass with soda all night, which gave Joey reason to be optimistic about the family's future. Garret had offered Oliver another chance at the farm, a part-time job as soon as he finished rehab—conditional, of course, on his continued sobriety.

She picked out her father's distinguished gray hair over in the corner where he appeared to tower over the mayor, more because of the power of his personality than his physical size. Joey noticed the lines crisscrossing his face, charting the ups and downs over forty years of running a farming operation and raising his family. He smiled at something Lincoln said and the energy flowed back into his face. She made a mental note to check with

Garrett to make sure her father was really stepping away from the operation and letting her eldest brother fully take the reins. He was more than capable and Harold knew it.

Joey gave in to her impulse to give her brother a hug.

"What's that for?" Garrett asked.

"For being one of the best brothers in the world."

"Now you realize that. Took you long enough." They laughed, just as his competition, her other brother Jimmy, pushed in between them.

"What about me?" Both his features and his voice made it clear the old resentments toward his older brother were forgotten. Joey wrapped an arm around him and kissed his cheek. "You are both the best big brothers a girl could have, in spite of everything."

They both looked at her, innocently. "What did we ever do?"

"Nothing I couldn't handle."

The doorbell rang, sending a rush of adrenalin through Joey's body. She nearly tripped over Duncan who was playing with a complicated building set on the floor behind her, and raced to the front door. As soon as she grasped the handle, she froze, trying to control the excitement she felt knowing who was on the other side.

When she swung it open, Fletch had Buddy in his arms, wrapped in a blanket. "Where do you want her?"

Duncan knew Buddy was coming home and was right behind her. "We've made up a hospital bed for her in here," he said, pointing the way.

Fletch looked at his booted feet, and then asked Joey, "Can you manage her? I have to go back to the car anyway."

When Joey reached out, he gently settled the dog in her arms, being careful not to twist the front leg with the cast. The dog whimpered a bit, sniffed Joey's hair and settled again.

"She's on painkillers so she's still pretty groggy," Fletch explained.

The kids had made a nest of blankets in a quiet corner of the living room where Joey settled her to rest peacefully. When Sylvia came in to check on things, Joey had to remind her to take her allergy medication. No point having her sneezing through their big holiday celebration. She heard the door open again and went out to meet Fletch and welcome him properly into the house. This time she threw herself at him and felt his strong arms wrap around her tightly.

"Merry Christmas to you too, sweetheart." She felt the chuckle in his chest and pushed away from him, a little embarrassed at her exuberance. "Sorry, I get a bit carried away at Christmas."

"Do you see me complaining? You can throw yourself into my arms any time you feel like it." The familiar grin softened his handsome face while the light from the foyer brought a twinkle to his eyes.

He had changed before coming over. He was commanding in his police uniform. In a suit, he was stunning and sophisticated. The gray wool cloth molded to his shoulders and wrapped smoothly across his broad chest, until it narrowed along his waist line. He looked like a man of the world. Joey flushed, conscious she was a small town girl while he'd experienced so much more in his lifetime.

As if reading her thoughts, Fletch touched her hair with the lightest of contact. She looked closely into his familiar face with that adorable grin. He took it as an invitation and brought his mouth down to brush across hers. She closed her eyes and savored the warmth and softness. The pressure increased as his arm came around her back. Her thoughts jumbled, started to drift away.

A rustling sound startled her. She noticed for the first time that a cardboard box lay on the floor at their feet with its flaps loosely closed. The rustling became more of a scratching and the source was inside.

"What is that?"

"Oh, the puppies are getting restless," he said.

"Puppies?" she gulped. "What puppies?"

"Rosebud's puppies. Vet says they're a couple of weeks premature but she had to deliver them because of the surgery."

Joey immediately dropped to her knees to open the box. "Oh lord, are they all right?"

"Perfectly. The car clipped Buddy's front leg."

She looked at the squirming little furballs writhing inside and her heart pounded.

"Puppies?" Duncan was leaning over her shoulder, wide-eyed with excitement.

"Dad, can I have Buddy's puppies for Christmas?"

Garrett laughed. "This is a bit of a surprise. Which one do you like, son?"

Duncan sighed. "Can't I have more than one?"

Lily knelt on the floor next to Duncan. "They're awfully cute. Maybe we should take two? They'd be good company for each other."

Joey laughed, knowing her big brother wouldn't be able to resist, but not wanting anyone to get too attached until the dogs were truly available for adoption.

So when Garrett nodded, she first explained the impound period to Duncan. "We all have to wait another few days to be sure no one is going to claim Buddy and her puppies." The light of excitement in his eyes dimmed. She stroked his soft cheek. "See how tiny her puppies are, Sweetie? They aren't strong enough yet to leave their mother, anyway. And, in the meantime, Buddy and her new little ones need our love and care, don't they?"

His angelic face glowed as he whispered, "I can still help Buddy look after them while she's sick. I can puppy-sit so she can rest, and bring them to her to have their meals since she can't walk, and everything."

Joey stood and ruffled his hair. "She'll be so glad to have you as a puppy-sitter. Let's take them in to their mommy now before they catch a chill."

Fletch picked up the box and followed them in to deposit the puppies with Buddy.

Everyone else was sitting at the table and Duncan was excitedly telling his grandfather about Santa's surprise delivery. Harold looked at Fletch and nodded his approval. Joey hoped it was for both the puppies and his decision to stay with her. They took the last two chairs at the big table, as everyone bowed their head to say grace. As the turkey, and potatoes and cranberry sauce, and all the rest of the trimmings made the rounds, Joey took in the scene around the table. It was unlike any she had ever experienced for the holidays. While she loved seeing her family together to celebrate Christmas, it was so much better to share the table with others, from the richest to the poorest of their home town. Baby Holly was being passed from one lap to another. Sammy and Ivy were holding hands as they patiently supervised the kids' table, which was no easy task with Duncan, Marcus and the youngest Belmonts completely distracted by the puppies nearby.

Garret broke her from her reverie by tapping his knife on a glass to get everyone's attention.

"I'm very proud of Duncan for managing to keep a secret for the last few hours—although I think getting a puppy for Christmas completely overshadowed his interest in Lily agreeing to marry us and join the Frost family."

Jimmy raised his glass. "Congratulations, bro," he said, sincerely. "I'll collect my kiss from the bride-to-be after dinner. But, let's not forget April and I got married first. I can still say I beat you at this one thing." He punched his brother in the shoulder, but their good humor was unmistakable.

Verna was rocking the baby as she fed her a bottle, and her face was transformed. Most of her troubles still lay ahead of her, yet her eyes glowed as she looked down at the tiny bundle in her arms. It was such a beautiful sight.

Fletch's hand covered hers, and he leaned close to her ear. "We'll make sure they stay together, sweetheart. Relationships that are meant to be just have a way of working out."

She had to wonder if they'd somehow stumbled onto the true meaning of Christmas, or had some little angel nudged them onto the right path.

Harold and Sylvia sat at either end of the table, happy to be sharing another holiday meal with multiple generations of their brood. Joey hadn't had a chance to ask her mother how her father had taken the changes to the traditional Frost family Christmas.

Harold Frost stood with a glass in hand. Nerves twitching, Joey followed his gaze around their holiday table trying to gauge his mood. He smiled at Garret and his new fiancée, then at Jimmy and his wife of only a week. From the stern look he gave Fletch, Joey thought her man would be receiving a serious talk before the end of the night—there was inherent risk in taking up with the only Frost daughter. But she wasn't worried. With her hand held firmly in his strong one, she was sure Fletch was up to the challenge.

She finally relaxed completely when she saw the warm smile her father sent to the Belmonts and the Lincolns. She had done the right thing...just as her parents had taught her to do from early childhood.

Her father cleared his throat. "This home provides safe shelter to our children, their wives and loved ones, as well as to the generations to follow and to those that have passed. We are ever thankful for the food on our table and the many blessings we have received through the year. We welcome our neighbors and friends, and their beautiful children, and wish them joy, peace and happiness in the year ahead, confident in the knowledge that they have the caring support of their community."

He raised his glass to deliver the traditional Frost family holiday toast. He paused and in that moment, Sylvia reassured Verna, as one of her boys emptied his glass in one gulp. "He's fine. It's just white grape juice."

Amid the laughter, everyone down to the

smallest child, lifted their glass and solemnly said, "God bless us every one."

The End

We hope you enjoyed A Frost Family Christmas. If you're not ready to leave the Frost Family and the town of Carol Falls, Vermont, check out the next two books in the series, available at most online bookstores.

MORE THAN A FEELING (BOOK FOUR)

by C. J. Carmichael

A dangerous twenty-year-old secret is about to be uncovered in the quaint Vermont town of Carol Falls, where not everyone is who they seem to be.

At first meeting, Spencer Frost appears to be a simple farmer who enjoys reading and quoting poetry. In fact he's a criminal law attorney from Boston on sabbatical at Frost Family Farm. When he meets Robin Redmond, the lovely new sales clerk at the local independent bookstore, he has no idea he's about to step into a drama to rival even his toughest legal case.

Robin moved to Carol Falls in pursuit of the man who destroyed her sister's life. Driven to face him—as well as her own guilt about her sister-- falling in love with Spencer is not part of her plans. But as they partner up to unravel the twisted truth behind the crime, she discovers love is the strongest weapon of all.

And if you're wondering what became of the woman who complicated Jim Frost's life, her past catches up with her in;

THE GREATEST GIFT (BOOK FIVE)

by Roxy Boroughs.

Heather Connolly has done some questionable things. But it was all to regain custody of her six-year-old daughter, Lottie. Finally together, Heather is now planning the perfect Christmas for her little girl.

Until police officers show up at the door and arrest Heather for robbery and arson.

Only one man can help prove her innocence. It's Zack Jones, a bouncer and volunteer firefighter...and the man she ran out on after their first and only night together.

Can he give her The Greatest Gift this Christmas, and once again unite Heather with her daughter? Or will Heather's past keep her from Lottie forever?

This story is a stand-alone sweet romance/cozy mystery. Series readers will enjoy catching up with town news and the latest happenings of the Frost Family...including a wedding.

About B.C. Deeks

B.C. Deeks writes heartwarming mysteries laced with a bit of romance, a little family and, often a wink of magic. THE HOLLY & THE IVY is one of the popular holiday themed stories in the Frost Family & Friends Series, written with CJ Carmichael and Roxy Boroughs. Brenda also has released WITCH IN THE WIND, the first book in her cozy paranormal mystery series, Fates of The Otherland, and is currently working on Book 2: MORTAL MAGIC. She has been published in numerous industry trade publications, such as Writers Market, and is a recognized expert on business issues for writers, as well as an award-winning technical writer. Born and raised in Newfoundland, an island off the east coast of Canada, Brenda now lives in the Rocky Mountains of Alberta, Canada. Look for Brenda's other titles at most online bookstores and at http://www.bcdeeks.com/.

Dedication and Acknowledgements

Police officers bring a special strength and dedication to their role of helping the people in their community. In writing this story, I wanted to illustrate what a home-grown, female officer might bring to her rural town, like our fictional Carol Falls (VT). I owe an enormous thank you to Devon McCrea of the Polson (MT) Police Department for sharing her expert knowledge of police procedures, and her experience as a police officer in her home town. That said, the actions and experiences of *my* characters are completely fictitious, and any errors are mine alone.

Thanks also to Clint Cottle, Assistant Chief, Polson (MT) Police Department, and Donna Earle, Chief of Records & Motor Carrier Services, Vermont Department of Motor Vehicles, who generously answered my questions for this story.

As always, there are no words to express how much I owe my writing partner, Roxy Boroughs, for her help with this book and my emerging writing career. Thanks for inviting me to participate in the Frost Family Christmas series—we both know that, without you, Fletch and Joey would never have had a romance.

My thanks also to author, C.J. Carmichael, for her generous advice and guidance throughout the Frost Family Christmas series.

I greatly appreciate, and relied upon, the eagle eyes of my beta readers, Ellen Murphy and authors Michelle Beattie, Suzanne Stengl and Dr. Paul W. Collins. And I wouldn't have been able to do this project without the constant support, encouragement, and *guy perspective* of my wonderful husband, Bruce Deeks, and my nephew, Alex Williams.

73323695R00107

Made in the USA
Columbia, SC
09 July 2017